P9-DMF-002

DISCARD

NIGHT JOURNEYS

Other Avon Camelot Books by
Avi

AMANDA JOINS THE CIRCUS • THE BARN
BEYOND THE WESTERN SEA, BOOK I: THE ESCAPE FROM HOME
BEYOND THE WESTERN SEA, BOOK II: LORD KIRKLE'S MONEY
BLUE HERON • ENCOUNTER AT EASTON
KEEP YOUR EYE ON AMANDA! • PUNCH WITH JUDY
ROMEO AND JULIET—TOGETHER (AND ALIVE!) AT LAST
SOMETHING UPSTAIRS • S. O. R. LOSERS
TOM, BABETTE, & SIMON: THREE TALES OF TRANSFORMATION
THE TRUE CONFESSIONS OF CHARLOTTE DOYLE
"WHO WAS THAT MASKED MAN, ANYWAY?"
WINDCATCHER

Tales from Dimwood Forest

POPPY
POPPY AND RYE
RAGWEED

Coming Soon in Hardcover

ERETH'S BIRTHDAY

Avon Flare Books

THE MAN WHO WAS POE • NOTHING BUT THE TRUTH
A PLACE CALLED UGLY
SOMETIMES I THINK I HEAR MY NAME

Avon Books are available at special quantity discounts for bulk purchases for sales promotions, premiums, fund raising or educational use. Special books, or book excerpts, can also be created to fit specific needs.

For details write or telephone the office of the Director of Special Markets, Avon Books, Inc., Dept. FP, 1350 Avenue of the Americas, New York, New York 10019, 1-800-238-0658.

AVI

NIGHT JOURNEYS

AN AVON CAMELOT BOOK

AVON BOOKS, INC.
1350 Avenue of the Americas
New York, New York 10019

Copyright © 1979 by Avi Wortis
Published by arrangement with William Morrow and Company, Inc.
Library of Congress Catalog Card Number 93-50233
ISBN: 0-380-73242-4
www.avonbooks.com

All rights reserved, which includes the right to reproduce this book or portions there-
of in any form whatsoever except as provided by the U.S. Copyright Law. For
information address Avon Books, Inc.

First Avon Camelot Printing: January 2000

CAMELOT TRADEMARK REG U S PAT OFF AND IN OTHER COUNTRIES, MARCA REGISTRADA,
HECHO EN U S A

Printed in the U.S.A.

OPM 10 9 8 7 6 5 4 3 2 1

If you purchased this book without a cover, you should be aware that
this book is stolen property. It was reported as "unsold and destroyed"
to the publisher, and neither the author nor the publisher has received
any payment for this "stripped book "

For Flossie and Jerry

NIGHT JOURNEYS

PART ONE

Morgan's Rock

1

My name is Peter York. I place here
before you the testimony of the great crisis in my life,
how it came to pass and what was the result.

In the fall of 1767, when I was twelve years of age,
my family perished by a fever. I alone, by God's
grace, was spared.

The evening of the funeral I was at the minister's
house, and while I sat alone by the kitchen table, a
meeting was held in the next room to decide what
was to be done with me.

The knowledge that they were debating my future
made me frantic, afraid as I was that none would have
me. For though I was willing to work, I had nothing
I could call my own save our mare, Jumper. Sitting
there I longed to cry, but dared not, lest they discover
me and think me an infant.

When at last the meeting grew still, I knew a decision had been reached. Sure enough, the door opened and the minister walked in.

"Peter," he announced, "here's Mister Shinn to take you."

I looked past the minister. There in the dim light of the candle I recognized the Quaker Everett Shinn, a man I knew only as the leader of the Quaker community and by the fact that he was the township's Justice of the Peace.

"Mister Shinn has kindly consented to take you in, Peter," said the minister. "If you promise to work hard, he'll treat you well."

"Yes, sir," I replied.

"Stand up and take his hand to mark the bargain," the minister prompted, a smile of charity glowing on his face.

I did as I was told. Mr. Shinn took my hand solemnly, peered at me, and nodded.

"Come, boy," urged the minister. "Have you nothing to say?"

I hardly knew what to speak. "Thank you, sir," I managed.

"Good!" cried the minister. "Mister Shinn, as ever, you're a credit to our township!"

In moments my horse was led out. Mr. Shinn mounted her and pulled me up behind him. Off we set in the dark for my new home and life. Mr. Shinn had not said one word.

2

Everett Shinn and his family lived in the Commonwealth of Pennsylvania, some sixty miles above Philadelphia, close to the Delaware River, between Well's Falls and the smaller falls, Galloper's Rift. The closest community was Coryell's Ferry. This was all sixteen miles north of Trenton, which lay across the river in Jersey Colony.

His family consisted, beside himself, of his young wife, Mistress Shinn, and their three children, all of whom were younger than I. He was a farmer, a man greatly respected in the community as proclaimed by his being chosen Justice of the Peace many terms.

A man in his sixties, he was heavy, even ponderous, and slow of foot. Of grave demeanor, never given to easy smiles, he spoke, when he did speak, with great care. In truth, it was silence that mostly ruled his tongue, a silence I found hard to fathom. It was a silence, moreover, that touched everything he did. It was so even when I observed him in his official function of Justice of the Peace presiding over the bodies of men who had drowned when they were swept over the falls. But then, not given to praise or condemnation, talking was a thing he did only with great reluctance.

With gray hair and pale features, he seemed at

times to be without emotion. All that he did was accomplished with a calm resolve and after much thought. This gave him a sense of dignity, which many found imposing. Beyond all else, Everett Shinn was a deeply religious man, a Quaker, given to piety and uprightness. The plainness of his garments, the somber hat he wore, announced that. Not that he was given to a great display of churchliness. On the contrary, his was a solitary way. And though he was Justice of the Peace, he was a Quaker first, rejecting all acts of violence.

If the truth be known—and I mean above all to tell the truth—I did not understand him.

I do not mean to suggest that he used me unkindly. Such was not the case. But I did not know why he had taken me in, other than because I would be required to work for him. I came to him with nothing but my ability to labor and the single inheritance of my horse.

It was through my horse, the only thing I claimed as mine, that all was to unravel.

3

By the spring of 1768 I had been with Mr. Shinn for about six months. Though it was a late spring, the green mist was fair upon the land and we had given thanks, for it had been a hard winter. Even so, the final chill was broken by two days of steady rain, which took whatever ice remained, though it did swell the river mightily. This was of concern, for when the winter breaks, there is always fear of flood. So while we were thankful for the warming rain, we also prayed that there would be no dangerous spring freshet.

When I think of what happened I understand that my story truly begins on the afternoon when the rains ceased. I had gone out squirrel shooting and had done well, returning to discover that Mr. Shinn had sent one of his young children on some trifling errand with the horse.

Jumper, the horse, was not a particularly fine beast, nor a great beauty. But I clung to her as the sole token of my previous life and lavished affection on her. Moreover, she was, or so I thought, mine and mine alone, and I presumed I had the right of her. This was not the case, however. Mr. Shinn, taking me into his family, took the horse as part of the bargain and used her at will without so much as a by my leave—as he had done that day. When I discovered this use, I protested. I also told Mr. Shinn that I thought there was sufficient reason for him to get a horse of his own so that Jumper could be rightfully returned to my exclusive charge.

Only after listening to me with his usual grave silence did he speak. "Thee are a full part of this family," he said. "I am the head of it. It's wrong for thee to dispute such a thing."

I persisted nonetheless, telling him that the horse was my sole inheritance and that while I did not oppose his use, he should not deny my ownership.

"A horse will cost as much as ten pounds," he said. "That we do not have. When we have the money— rather, *if* we have the money—I shall consider thy request."

And that was all he said.

There was nothing more I could do, though I confess I greatly resented what I thought was a putting-off.

That night, when I had gone to bed in the loft where I slept alone, I could not sleep. What with the fresh air, the sounds of spring, and my churning over the great matter of the horse, I lay awake listening to the rising river, thinking of nothing but how I might get money enough so that I might have my horse back. As I lay—it was perhaps nine o'clock, and Mr.

Shinn and his wife had retired—there was a great thumping on the front door.

"Mister Shinn! Mister Shinn!" came an urgent call.

Bolting from my bed, I looked out through the small loft window onto the yard. There I saw five horses, four men in their saddles. The fifth man was presumably knocking on the door. Two of the riders I recognized, Isaac Waterford and Richard Pall, who carried a bright torch. I did not know the other two men. All had rifles in their hands.

It was an unusual sight, made more unusual by the presence of the strangers. Knowing that something of importance must have occurred, I hastened to the loft ladder, climbed halfway down, and looked on.

Mr. Shinn, slowly tucking his blouse into his britches, opened the door to a greatly excited Nathaniel Dempsy, a man I knew from the township. Mr. Dempsy was Mr. Shinn's oath-taker, the one who administered legal oaths to people since Mr. Shinn's religion kept him from doing so.

"Mister Shinn," he cried. "Here's an alarum been given!"

"For what? For whom?" returned Mr. Shinn, who refused to raise his voice no matter what the occasion or how provoked he became.

"A gentleman's come, Mister Shinn, a Mister John Tolivar from Trenton, telling us about his escaped bondsmen—*two* escaped bondsmen! He thinks they may cross the river hereabouts."

Escaped bondsmen! It happened from time to time, and we were bound to know of it because Mr. Shinn lived so close to the river, which those who escaped often tried to cross. More important, as Justice of the Peace, Mr. Shinn was obliged to know and render all assistance.

Bondsmen, I should explain, were men, women, and even children who had been brought from England or Europe under contract for their labor. Some were apprentices. Some were indentured servants or redemptionists, while others were transported felons. All were obliged to work for periods of time by those who owned their labor, after which time—if they still lived—they were set free. But often they would attempt to free themselves. The Delaware River being a boundary between Jersey and Pennsylvania, it was a line many of them sought to cross. If they were caught and returned to their rightful masters, those who caught them would get a good reward—sometimes in hard coin—for bondsmen were of great value.

"If they're heading Easton way," continued Nathaniel Dempsy, "they might well come hereabouts."

"Does thee know if they had a horse?" asked Mr. Shinn.

"I don't think so. You'd best speak to the gentleman yourself," said Dempsy, gesturing toward one of the strangers.

Refusing to be hurried, Mr. Shinn pulled on his boots, coat, and hat. "I presume," he said, "there's a reward, or thee would not have come at such a time."

"Twelve pounds, Mister Shinn," agreed Dempsy in an excited whisper, not hearing the rebuke in Mr. Shinn's remark. "*Twelve pounds* he's offered for them."

Mr. Shinn shook his head. "I'll join thee soon enough," he said, and withdrawing quickly, shut the door behind Dempsy.

The moment I understood what had occurred, the thought of the reward caught my mind and inflamed it. Twelve pounds! *There* was the needed horse! Hurriedly I dressed and dropped out of the loft.

"I'll go too," I announced eagerly, taking the gun down from its place.

Mr. Shinn paused in his preparations and looked across at me. "Bondsmen are not squirrels," he said sharply. "Put that gun back."

I did as he told me, but I still confronted him. "There's a reward," I said. "You spoke of the money you needed to buy yourself a horse."

Avoiding the presumption of my statement, he said,

MEMORIAL SCHOOL LIBRARY
81 CENTRAL AVENUE
HULL, MASSACHUSETTS 02045

11

"I'm going because I'm obliged. Thee are not. We'll be gone all night, perhaps more. We may not even find them. They don't give up easily."

"I shan't mind it any more than you do," I retorted as I got my jacket.

Mistress Shinn had by this time gotten up, but he paid no attention to her.

"Thee are too young," he said to me.

Stung by his words, I hotly protested. "You require man's work from me."

He studied me for a long moment, then, at last, nodded his acceptance. "We'll be back in time," he said to his wife, and opening the door he led the way, a lantern in his hand.

Once outside I had my first look at John Tolivar, the gentleman from Trenton, and his companion, a servant who held a torch. I saw instantly from his clothing, and from the wig tied with bright ribbons, that Mr. Tolivar was a wealthy man. He was positively elegant, in great contrast to the drabness that suited Mr. Shinn. In his hands was a fine rifle.

"John Tolivar," said Mr. Shinn, offering his hand. "My name is Everett Shinn, Justice of the Peace. May I be of service to thee?"

"I thank you, sir," returned Mr. Tolivar with great civility. "It's much what that man has already related. I've lost two servants, transported felons, and one of them branded at that. I mean to have them back. They cost me enough and they owe me years of labor. I'm offering twelve pounds reward, sir. As Justice of the Peace your help is sincerely requested."

"If I can aid thee lawfully without killing, I shall," replied Mr. Shinn.

"Not to worry," said Mr. Tolivar with a tolerant smile. "I want no murders on my soul. A dead servant is no good to me or, I suppose, to anyone." This joke brought appreciative laughter from the others.

Mr. Shinn was not smiling, however. He merely nodded to me, and I hurried off to saddle Jumper.

"Tell me who the bondsmen are," I heard him request as I went off.

As quickly as I could, I saddled Jumper and brought her to them. The party was waiting impatiently and Mr. Shinn, if anything, was graver than before. With some effort, he mounted, then held out his hand to pull me up behind him.

As I mounted, Mr. Tolivar leaned over the neck of his horse and observed me closely. "Is the boy going too?" he asked.

Mr. Shinn nodded. "I thought him too young myself, but he wishes to go."

"Good!" exclaimed Mr. Tolivar. "He looks lively enough. And might he not be of particular service, Mister Shinn? But I confess I can't see what good either of you will be without guns."

"I try not to use them," replied Mr. Shinn patiently.

"They give good signals, don't you think?" suggested Mr. Tolivar with slight mockery.

But Mr. Shinn, showing no offense, merely nodded and dispatched me for our gun. As I went, I glowed with pleasure at the gentleman's remark concerning me. How it contrasted with that made by Mr. Shinn! It made me more resolved than ever to show him what I could do.

When I returned with the gun and its accoutrements, I was once more pulled up behind Mr. Shinn.

Satisfied, Mr. Tolivar took his leave, announcing that he would return home and await word from us or any of the other parties he had alerted.

"Be good enough to send for me when you can tell me something," he requested. "And Godspeed!" Wheeling about, he and his servant dashed off.

We waited till their torchlight dimmed, nobody saying a word, though I had nothing but admiration for the man. Once Mr. Tolivar left, our party, led by Richard Pall's fluttering torch, moved northward on River Road in search of the runaways.

4

As we got underway, my first thought was to ask Mr. Shinn who the escaped men were and what they looked like, for I had missed that information while I was away saddling Jumper. I saw that Mr. Shinn was in no mood to talk, so I resolved to keep my questions for later, concentrating instead on the road ahead.

Our way was through the night. Mr. Pall's torch made a tunnel of light in which we moved, the singular brilliance making all beyond seem much darker. Against the walls of leafless trees our shadows stalked behind us so that our little band seemed double in number.

River Road, on which we traveled, was normally a fairly wide road that ran parallel to the river some seventy yards or so inland. But after all the winter snows and more recent rains, the road was nothing more than a bed of mud, and it was impossible to go fast. Nonetheless, we continued to ride for about a mile until we stopped at Dewar's Landing, at which point we drew the horses close in order to make plans.

"If they haven't a boat, and that's not likely according to this Tolivar," said Dempsy, speaking softly, "there are only a few places they can get across. Not likely to swim, are they?"

Richard Pall volunteered to say that swimming the river was close to impossible.

"But they can't be too bright, trying to cross with the river rising," put in Waterford.

"Aye, they may know no better," murmured Dempsy.

"If they do get horses," put in Pall, "they'll go farther north, and we'll never get them. Reach Easton, and they might as well be free. But look here, there's only four good fording places: Bull's Island, Morgan's Rock, Old Orchard, and Dewar's Landing. If each of us takes a post, and we keep our rifles ready, we can send a signal if we spy them."

"I'm for that," agreed Waterford. "We won't be so far apart that we can't join up if we need to. Five against two should make it sure," he said, including me in the count, to my great pride. "What do you think, Mister Shinn?"

"I don't think anyone will cross at Morgan's Rock this time," he said, breaking his silence.

"One did two years ago," Pall reminded him.

"Aye," said Mr. Shinn. "But it was summer and the river was low." He looked about at the other men. "I suppose thee would like me there," he said, deliberately choosing the least likely spot.

This indeed was what they wanted. Very quickly thereafter, they agreed about who would man the other places; Dempsy chose to remain at Dewar's

Landing, while Pall and Waterford took the remaining two locations.

We started off again. Mr. Shinn took the lead with his lantern hooded, moving slowly, for the ground if anything was worse and the horses were unsure. No one spoke. Only the plodding sounds of the horses broke the constant wash of the still rising river.

Very soon we picked our way to Old Orchard, where Waterford was to watch. He took some flame from Mr. Shinn's lantern in order to light his own, then drifted away. We watched his spot of light move through the dark until we could see it no more.

Continuing north, we left Mr. Pall opposite Bull's Island. Then Mr. Shinn and I moved through the dark toward Morgan's Rock.

At the spot on the road closest to it, we dismounted. I led Jumper by her bridle down the path while Mr. Shinn kept the lamp, which was rather careless, I thought, for we thus showed a light. Down at the river's edge, we went opposite the island known as Morgan's Rock.

At that point the Delaware River is fairly wide, almost a quarter of a mile, wider than anywhere else for some miles north or south. There in the river lies Morgan's Rock, set at unequal distances from the river's banks: fifty yards from the Pennsylvania side and perhaps three hundred or so from Jersey.

A narrow island, Morgan's Rock is much in the

shape of a teardrop, its pointed end to the south. At the northern end a mass of rock thrusts against the river's flow like the prow of a great ship, making the river split into two different paths.

On the eastern—Jersey—side of the island the water runs wide and fairly shallow, making it wild and fierce. On the western—Pennsylvania—side, it's the reverse. There the narrow channel runs to a greater depth but is quiet as church. But on that side a line of broken rock juts halfway into the river: the dangerous Finger Falls.

Thus, while one side of the island is rough and fast, there is no obstruction; the other side is soft but obstructed. Boats coming down the river must decide which route to take. To the unknowing, the silent side looks easier. To those who know, the rough side is the wiser choice. Too late a decision is the greatest danger of all, for at the dividing point, where the rock stands, the river is at its worst, tearing itself like mad dogs in battle. Many a boat has broken there; and men have drowned. The island's very name—Morgan—recalls a man who so drowned.

The land directly behind the rock itself is an island clear of water. The northern section, some sixty yards or more, is solid and fertile, being heavily overgrown with trees, bushes, and whatever else can grow there. Indeed, the foliage is so thick that it's hard to enter. Moreover, it holds masses of logs and branches, hurled up on the island by the rolling waters around the rock.

The island's southern end is but an ever narrowing strip of sand and silt, which lengthens and shortens depending on the river's height.

Curiously, the island is known as a good place to ford the river. Indeed, it *is* a good place, but only when the river is low, such as might occur in summer. Then one can drive a wagon across the shallow side, cross the island, and float across the narrow channel.

At one place near the middle the sand and trees comingle. Mostly open and easy to cross, it was there we meant to take our watch.

5

We tied Jumper loosely to a tree, but kept her saddle on, not knowing when, or if, we would be called upon to use her.

The place to which we had come was a little landing area. There, a small flat-bottomed boat was kept, which belonged to a man who fished for shad. A low-sided craft (no more than eight inches in height), it was steady but so easily swamped as to make it useless for anything except the calm waters we intended to cross. At the bottom of the boat lay the two poles used to push it.

Having set the lantern at one end of the boat, I fixed the rifle on Mr. Shinn's back, then each of us took up a pole. Standing on either side we edged off into the channel and began to push.

As I have said, the western channel of the island is far calmer than the eastern. Even so, with the water rising, the river ran swiftly. We had to work in unison, Mr. Shinn and I, or else the boat would most certainly have spun.

Beginning at the prow, we pushed the poles into the river bottom, and firmly holding the poles, walked toward the stern. This moved the boat forward and kept it on an even course. We reached the other side in moments.

I leaped ashore and tied the boat's rope securely to a nearby tree.

"The water's still rising," I said to Mr. Shinn.

"That will make it easier for us," he answered.

"Why?" I asked.

"I'll show thee." Still holding his lantern carelessly, he led me over the narrow width of the island across the slight rise in its center. We stood then upon the eastern side.

It was yet night, but the high half-moon was bright and unobstructed so that I could look across. The Jersey side was a black mass of trees. The river before us, swollen and shapeless, had flecks of foam that caught the moonlight, revealing the water's speed.

What I saw made my heart sink. Anyone attempting to cross the river there and then would have to be a fool. He would be swept away, never to reach the island.

"We'll win no rewards here," I complained.

Mr. Shinn shrugged.

Swinging about, he moved a few feet up the island's rise to a place where we could look down on the river, keep our feet from getting wet, yet lean comfortably against the trees.

"Now," he whispered, settling his back and trimming the lantern to a lower light so that the night seemed to come that much closer. "Let us wait and hope that no one comes. Thee wished to come, Peter. Look to thy silence."

6

Despite Mr. Shinn's reluctance to move quickly, our coming to Morgan's Rock had meant a certain amount of activity. But once we set in to do our waiting, it grew hard for me. Mr. Shinn had the patience to sit and work his mind in silent ways. Not I. Perhaps I was too young. The thought of doing nothing made me impatient as I sat there, my back against an ever-hardening tree, the high roar of the river filling my ears with monotonous wash.

I tried to think of ways to keep awake, beating my hands on the ground and the like. At one point I took up our rifle and exercised myself by rechecking its loading, and keeping it ready on my knees. Even that proved insufficient. I felt compelled to break the silence.

"What kind of men do you think they are?" I ventured.

Mr. Shinn hesitated, and when he did speak, it was with obvious reluctance. "This John Tolivar did not say much," he answered evasively. "Let's hope we never see them."

"He called them felons," I persisted, my mind filled with lurid images of cutpurses, scamps, and rogues.

"Aye," he said. "Transported here from England as an act of King's mercy."

"Is it not a mercy then?" I asked.

"Branded on the thumb," he said slowly, "they choose between the gallows and America, owing men like this Tolivar many years of labor. It's hard to know if that's a choice."

I found his mournful tone annoying. "They should be thankful they're alive and not try to escape," I suggested.

"People prefer their freedom," he returned.

"Even against the law?" I challenged.

"The law's a chain that keeps all as one," he said. "But mind, it's still a chain."

"We'll catch them," I said with high bravado. "We need the money. You said so yourself."

"I would not exult so much."

Feeling his criticism unfair, I returned in kind. "But you're Justice of the Peace," I said. "You can't have it both ways."

"No," he agreed, "I can't. Though I can pray they go another way."

This remark frustrated me so that I spoke a venturesome thing. "Or both ways," I taunted. "Like the taking of oaths. You hold oath-taking sinful, but you allow Mister Dempsy to swear them as you look the other way. Perhaps it's wrong for you to be Justice of the Peace."

Abruptly, he shifted around, and even in the dim light I saw his anger. In an instant it seemed to ebb, and he retreated to his private, silent thoughts.

I thought even less of him for saying naught, certain that if *I* held his position, *I* would not refuse its gifts. What was an escaped man but a breaker of the law? I asked myself. Why come out to hunt and then pray not to see the catch? All effort and no reward! In my mind I judged Mr. Shinn a hypocrite for believing one thing and acting another. But prudently I only thought these things; I said no more.

Instead I tried to picture what the felons would be like; big, strong, reckless men, I was certain. But *I* would be without fear! Why, I asked myself, did I not have a gun? And in my eagerness I lifted it and sighed down its barrel.

"Put up thy gun," Mr. Shinn said softly, taking it from my hands. "I use no gun against any man."

Stung anew, I barely kept my tongue, but renewed my vow to show myself, and him, just what I could do.

7

Close to five o'clock in the morning the darkness became suffused with light, the chill of the air giving way to the damp warmth that was the morning's dawn. Before us the river churned up a steaming mist so that the view of the other side was broken, filled in, and broken yet again. The river, clearly, was much higher.

"Here, Peter," said Mr. Shinn. "Thee should go home."

"I want to stay," I replied.

"Thee are tired," he said. "I won't think less of thee for going. There are no signals yet. I doubt they'll come at all."

"I'm staying," I repeated, angry at him for suggesting I was weak.

"Then walk about a bit," he urged. "Sitting puts a weight upon one's eyes."

I did in fact feel stiff, so I stood up.

"Just put the gun farther up," he said, handing it to me. "It's likely to dampen here."

Taking the gun, I went higher on the island's back. Then I turned to the southern, sandy part, but decided nothing was worth looking at there. The northern section with its thick foliage and close trees held a greater fascination. Moreover, I thought to climb Morgan's Rock, knowing it would offer a splendid view. I took a step in that direction.

"Leave the rifle here," Mr. Shinn called. "And cover the powder with this." He handed up his linen handkerchief.

Irritated that he felt compelled to remind me, I took the cloth, and after placing the gun in the dry cleft of a tree, covered it as he had said. Then I moved on.

I proceeded along the center of the island, working my way through the trees. It was not easy. They grew very close, their countless branches seeming to have sought out every tongue of light that managed to slip through. Even the roots were much exposed. When I did not trip or have a branch slap me in the face, I stepped into a marshy place. In one spot I all but lost a boot and had to pull it free with both my hands.

Nonetheless I made progress. Soon I caught a glimpse of the rock itself, rising in the river like a mountain. It was, of course, nothing of the kind; for it was no more than fifteen feet in height. But in the morning mist it did seem huge.

The vegetation began to thin. The ground grew higher, harder; fewer things grew, and what did grow was stunted. Soon I was on the lowest part of the rock. There I turned toward the water, for the mist was rising quickly and I wanted to see where the water churned the most. When I reached the water's edge I sat upon a stone, where the mist gave way to a fine, constant spray. Very soon I was completely damp, though I felt no splash. Water ran down my face.

With every passing moment the day grew brighter. The Jersey side stood out with great clarity, although here and there were what seemed like clouds upon the banks. The scene took my fancy and held my eyes.

It was then I saw it.

At first I wasn't sure what it was. Across the way, directly opposite where I sat, on the Jersey shore, I had spied a flash of white. Then, whether hidden by trees, mist, or design, it was gone again.

It was enough to make me rise from my place.

Even so, I knew that the dawn, the mist, and the white-capped water might have confused me. I sat down again and waited to see if the flash of white returned.

It did. Something *was* there, but I could no more be sure as to what it was than I'd been before. It didn't matter! My fancy filled in the spot with notions that I had found the dangerous men we were looking for. It made my heart race fair.

Yet, my hope quickly went again, for I was still not completely convinced by what I'd seen.

When the flashing white appeared once more against the dark, I was mortally certain that someone was there. I stood, poised to run back to where Mr. Shinn waited, and even took a step. Then, to my surprise, the report of a gun rang out. Responding instantly, I leaped from my place and began to hurry back. As I ran, a second report sounded. Only then was I struck by the realization that the signal of the sighting was coming *not* from Mr. Shinn, but from much farther south.

8

It had been hard enough working my way through that tangled mass of trees and weeds when I only had an aimless purpose; it was much worse as I hurried back. I must have slipped twenty times.

"Peter!" I heard Mr. Shinn's urgent cry.

"I'm coming!" I returned, relieved that he was waiting for me. I tried to push on faster, and that is where I came to grief. Down went my foot into a boggle hole, catching me unaware and at full tilt. I started to fall, and as was only natural, put out my hands. This broke my fall, but instantly I felt a sharp pain in my left arm. I made myself come up at once, though it hurt my arm to push. Anxiously I moved my fingers, wrist, and arm. I saw at once that I had broken nothing. But the sprain, or whatever it was, was no less hurtful.

"Peter!" came Mr. Shinn's call again.

"Here!" I cried, and started to run again. Without thinking, I held my left arm—the one that had been hurt—with my right.

In moments I burst into an open space between the trees and saw Mr. Shinn waiting impatiently in the little boat, both his pole and mine in hand. I leaped aboard.

"I'm sorry," I said, taking the pole he thrust at me.

"I think the signal was from about a mile south," he said as we began to work across the channel. "That should be Isaac Waterford."

"Do you think he's seen them?" I asked.

"He has, or at least he's heard some news we need to know," he replied. "What's happened to thy arm?" he abruptly asked when he realized I was not managing as well as I had before.

"I fell," I simply said. "That's all."

"Broken?"

"No. I'm sure it's not."

"In pain?"

"Not so much," I replied, somehow feeling that if I told him otherwise it would be an admission of a fault.

He said nothing but worked his pole as I worked mine, though as we crossed he kept observing me.

Another gunshot sounded from the south. We looked up.

"What's that mean?" I asked.

"They must have them cornered," he surmised. "They'll need me quickly."

After a few more shoves, we reached the shore. He jumped off and I followed. Hurriedly I tied the boat, then ran for Jumper, who had been waiting patiently. Mr. Shinn swung onto the saddle first, then held his arm out for me to mount. Suddenly he held off.

"Where's thy rifle?" he demanded.

The gun! I had left it on the island!

He read the answer in my eyes. "Thee has left it," he said, shaking his head. I would have felt better had he scolded.

"With a sore arm and thy rifle gone, thee will not be of much use, Peter. Can thee get back to the island and fetch the gun without me?"

Realizing my own foolishness, I could hardly argue with him. "Of course," I said.

"Then best do it," he said. "Thee can find thy way home on foot. There will be other times to prove thy manhood. I must go on. I'm wanted."

Wasting no further words, he turned Jumper about and trotted up the path toward the road. With a final look and wave he hurried out of sight.

I knew it was my own fault. I should have kept the watch. I should not have left the gun where I did. I should not have tripped and hurt my arm. All the same I grew sorry for myself, and not a little angry; anything rather than the feeling of foolishness that was also mine. I chided: *He* had been slow enough in coming to the island *with* me. And once the alarum had sounded, how quick he was to get away alone.

30

But, for all my ruminating I had acted like an ass.

There was no choice. I turned back toward the river.

The morning was full. The sun, though not in any way hot, poured down through the trees, bright enough to make me blink. The river, its early mist blown over, was blue and deep, but ran faster than before.

Feeling no urgency, only petulance, I walked slowly to the boat, untied it, stepped aboard, and picked up one of the poles. I was just about to push off when I moved my left arm and felt the pain anew. I had forgotten that.

Deciding that I had acted foolish enough for one day, I thought I should consider what I was about before I moved off alone. There is a big difference in poling a boat with one person than with two.

Accordingly, I looked more closely at the channel I had to cross. It was no more than a hundred feet wide and so much calmer than the other side of the island that it seemed but a flowing pool. But it *was* moving, and I took note of that.

Stepping off the boat I fetched up a bit of rotten wood and flung it in the water to see how fast it moved. It pulled away quickly. From the speed with which it went I knew that it would be impossible to go straight across as we had done before. I had to go at an angle.

Now more certain of what I was about, I stepped into the boat again and pushed off with the pole planted on the downriver side of the craft. Then I walked it back. The old boat moved with ease. Too much ease. At once I felt the boat push against the pole itself. Turning partly about, I leaned heavily with both my arms on the pole, intending to slow the rush. As I did so, a sharp pain ran through my arm, and without meaning to, I pulled it quickly back. The boat, now fully caught in the river's flow, swung around the pole speedily, as if the pole were a pivot.

Hastily I lifted the pole high and tried to plant it again on the downstream side, but in such a way as to break the movement of the craft. I thrust it down hard, seeking the river bottom. But the boat had moved so quickly from the shore, and the river was so much higher, that the bottom was not where I thought it would be. Instead, I plunged the pole into what felt like an abyss. Down I went, falling flat upon my belly while the pole sprang from my hand. I lunged at it, even touched it with a finger, but this only caused it to fall away more. It was gone.

Instantly, I spun around and grabbed the remaining pole. That time I stayed on my knees and frantically plunged the pole downward. The boat hurled against it, breaking it in two with a cracking snap that stung my hands.

I was adrift.

Had I my wits about me at that point I could have easily jumped over the side, for I don't think the water was above my head. But my sense of surprise, if not shock, allowed me to do nothing of the kind. I merely sat there stupidly, watching aghast as the boat began to gain in speed.

When I fully understood what I had done I was petrified—not because of any danger to myself, for I did not see that yet—but because I had added one more item to my lengthening list of follies.

That self-centered thought gave way to a concern far greater: not only was I rapidly moving down river, but I was also moving past the island, fast approaching its end. Beyond, in the churning river, lay the Finger Falls.

PART TWO

The River

1

Even though I fully understood how dangerous was my situation, it did not keep me from making my next mistake—an attempt to *reason* what I might do. Instead of thinking, I simply should have leaped off the boat and hauled it back to shore. But, unwilling to do anything else that might be wrong, unable to trust myself, I sat back and thought even as I was being swept along.

While so preoccupied, I rapidly passed the island's lower end, and in moments I was full upon the heaving river. I knew well the danger I was in; out from the protection of the soft channel water I was tumbled about in earnest, and in a moment might be flung against the Finger Falls. I knew now how fast the water moved, far faster than I had reckoned from the land. Such was the river's constant hiss that it seemed like I had fallen upon a living thing. No amount of swimming would now bring me to shore.

The boat itself, being flat-bottomed, lay upon the

water like the lid on a boiling pot, tilting back and forth. Water spurted in and out at will, smacking against the low walls of the boat, causing one side board to loosen.

As the boat began to rock ever more precariously, I lay down, spreading my arms and legs as wide as possible so that my weight should not tip the craft one way or another, daring to lift my head only from time to time to see where I was going. Yet, lying there, rapidly sweeping toward the falls, I knew I had to act. It was the loose board that gave me back my life. Carefully, without raising myself to any height, I reached out and pulled it. The old board came free with ease, and since the water was already splashing over the low craft, it made no real difference in the amount of water that continued to crash over me.

Holding the board in both my hands, I crawled forward as much as I dared, then dangled the board into the river as if it were a rudder. Pushing it deeply down into the water, yet holding it firmly, I found that by turning it, the boat could be made to veer off to one side or another. Thus, after a crude fashion, I could steer. That was all I needed. As I was also moving down, I began to cross the river in zigzag fashion. I knew, then, that I could get to Jersey safely, if not to the Pennsylvania side. In any case, I could avoid the falls.

I cannot say for certain how long it took me to get across; in the end, my ordeal did not last more than moments. Though I felt I wasn't moving fast enough, the Jersey side suddenly loomed very large.

The finale of my voyage, short as it was, caught me unprepared. Perhaps it was because I had been laying low and could gauge neither my speed nor my position. Just as I thought I had reached quieter water and the safety of the shore, the boat smashed headlong into a projecting rock.

So unexpected was the jolt that I dropped the rudder board, totally losing control of the boat's direction. Thus free, it swung about with such speed that it took my breath away even while the vessel heaved itself against another stone. This second blow, falling broadside, produced a great splintering as the boat began to break up.

Falling apart, it became caught in the eddies of the tumbling shallows, shooting itself from rock to rock, smashing more each time it struck. In my panic, I leaped off, thinking the water shallow. It was deeper than I thought, being up to my chest. I had tried as I jumped to hold what remained of the boat, but the shock of the sudden plunge into water made me lose that final grip.

What remained of the boat, much lighter by my leave-taking, rose high atop the water, sprang away, dashed about some rocks, then tore itself into many bits, all of which whisked down the river and out of sight.

I stood there, panting, chest deep in water, watching the pieces go, as like to cry as not. Could I do nothing right! Now I had lost the boat, and whose boat it was I did not know. I watched for as long as I could, cursing myself with every swearing word that I had ever heard spoke, as if the words were some magic charms and the energy I gave them could, somehow, return the boat to me. But it was gone, and I was only more a sinner.

Wearily, I turned my face to the shore and began to wade out. Even at that I didn't have it right; I slipped once more and received yet another soaking of my spirits.

I climbed up on the Jersey shore as disgusted with myself as one could be. There I was—wet clear through, cold, without a boat, and farther than ever from retrieving the gun.

My left arm began to throb. The pain seemed worse than before, no doubt because in my anxiousness I simply had forgotten the soreness and had used the arm in violation of the hurt.

I made myself sit down upon a rock. From there I gazed at the rushing river, holding my arm and giving myself up to self-pity at my plight. I was hungry, too; I had not eaten since the night before.

Still, I took comfort in such warmth as there was,

taking off my boots and pouring the water out of them. I wrung my shirt, too, giving the river back much of the water it had loaned.

The thing I felt most was shame! I who had so wanted to prove myself. What I longed for most was home, yet I felt I could not just go back.

The easiest thing for me to have done was to go to the ferry at Well's Falls, only a few miles to the south. But that way, though simple, was hard for me. I would have to explain to the ferryman why I couldn't pay the threepence it took to cross. From him, my story would go everywhere. The thought of that confession and the mocking gossip that would ensue from it was too much for me to bear.

Then, too, I was determined to retrieve the rifle. The loss of it would rightly anger Mr. Shinn. I had seen but a touch of his anger; I wanted to see no more.

What was uppermost in my mind—gun, pride, or fear—I do not know. But I was determined to regain the first two before I returned home.

The sun grew warmer, my clothing dried, and the chill I had felt dropped off. But I continued to think how I might get back to Morgan's Rock without benefit of ferry.

In due time I conceived a plan. It was this: had I not come across the river with ease? I had. It had been quick, but there had been no real danger, and save for the last few moments when I'd not been alert, I suffered no real harm. Getting wet and breaking the boat had been caused—so I believed—only by a lack of attention on my part. Could I not regain the island simply by going in reverse? That is, if I went far enough upstream, above the island, and floated down, perhaps on a log, could I not regain the island—and my gun and my pride?

It was a simple plan. Moreover, I felt sure, a safe one. I had conquered the river once; I could do it twice. My sense of shame was stronger than any current. I was determined to try.

Putting on my shirt and still-damp boots, I started to move upriver. Just then, a fusillade of shots rang out somewhere below. It put me in mind again of what I'd all but forgotten, the escaped men. I shook my head over the ill luck and gross misfortune that had kept me from that hunt, the reward, the horse. How far away it all seemed!

Feeling uniquely put upon, I continued my way along the Delaware.

2

Determined to put my plan into effect as soon as possible, I moved quickly north. Though it was a flat area, my view was often impaired by the many trees that stood close to the higher-than-normal water. In my ride I had gone no farther than a half mile to the south, however, so Morgan's Rock was never completely out of view. I paid particular attention to the location of the island as I walked, and not thinking about much else, I was brought up short by a momentary sight of that flashing white I had earlier noticed from the island.

As you will recall, when first I spied the whiteness I thought it to be one of the runaways. I knew now that it could not be, for the signal shots had come from far below. Still I was curious to know what, or who, was causing the flash of white.

Despite my desire to hurry, I resolved to investigate. Even so, my chief concern was that it might be someone I knew. I did not wish to be observed, lest I have to explain how I came to be on the Jersey side. I moved inland, therefore, away from the river, hiding behind whatever thick growth would cover me.

Hidden from view, I proceeded north again in a much more cautious manner, trying to make little noise, though I suppose any sound would have been overwhelmed by the noise of the river.

I constantly peered toward the river in hopes of seeing the white again. But since I had seen it only briefly, I was not even certain of the exact place.

When I did catch sight of it again, it was but a glimpse on my left. Down I went on my hands and knees and crept forward so that I could gain a better view. It was not long before I saw what it was.

To my great relief the whiteness belonged to neither man nor boy. It was a girl. Any fears that my follies would be thrown up at me melted away.

I saw her first from the back. She was standing on the shore looking out on the river, partly obscured by a rock. I could see that she was not very tall, shorter even than myself. Judging from the Shinn children's height, I took her to be perhaps eleven years of age. Her shirt—for it was a glimpse of its cloth that I had first seen—was a poor thing, less white than dirty gray. It was old, too, and even at a distance I could see that it was torn. Her skirt was made of some dark cloth; it was ill-fitting, far too big for her, and in high need of repair.

She was partially hidden by a biggish stone near the water's edge. She seemed, however, to be doing nothing more than staring at the river.

She stood there for a while, then turned about and moved a few paces, looking toward the south from time to time. Only when she turned north did I see her face.

Her brows were dark, her mouth full, though her face was thin. Her hair, which was also dark and without benefit of bonnet, hung below her shoulders in disarray.

What mattered most for the sake of my pride was my certainty that I had never seen her before. Nor, I presumed, did she know me.

That I did not know her was hardly strange. After all, we lived on the Pennsylvania side of the river. While I knew most families thereabouts who lived between Coryell's Ferry and Howell's Ferry, those who lived on the Jersey side might well have lived in England for all I knew.

Watching from my place of hiding, and seeing the way she paced with hesitant back and forth steps and a constant looking across, put me in mind of a puppy fearful of entering a stream but knowing it must do so all the same. I was certain she wanted to cross the river.

I looked past her and observed that we were both opposite Morgan's Rock. It was that, I think, which convinced me more than anything else that she wanted to cross. From where she was standing, she could not be sure that the island was truly an island. All she could see was that it was the nearest reach across the water.

Then, too, perhaps because of my own predicament, I felt kinship with her. We were both, or so I thought, trying to cross the river. She was younger than I, and a girl, so I felt superior to her, which at the moment was balm to me. It was thus easy for me to go further: thinking of my plan and my sore arm, I thought she might be of help to me. Two might be able to get across easier than one.

Watching from my place of concealment, I saw her wade into the water as far as her knees, as if thinking she might walk across. The river broke against her and she all but fell, throwing her hands out for balance. Quickly she retreated to the shore and stood there helplessly.

It made me smile to see her so. Clearly there was no way she could get across. It was obvious to me she could not swim.

Back on the shore, she sat on a rock as if thinking to find a way. My sense of superiority grew and grew. Had *I* not crossed? Did *I* not know how to cross again? *I* did!

Certain that I could get her to help me, I decided to reveal myself. I rose up to a full view and gave a shout of greeting.

3

My sudden appearance and call startled her greatly. She leaped about, looked at me, and would, I believe, have run away if she had not seen at once that I was no more than a boy. Even so, she seemed unsure what to do between running and staying, but watched me closely as I came forward as simply as I could. My calm manner seemed to set her mind at rest somewhat.

As I came closer I was able to see her face more clearly and to observe something of her person. What I saw was a puzzle to me, struck as I was by a look of age that belied her height and form. A look of fear was there, and a hardness, too. There was no softness such as I knew from the Shinn children. Indeed, when I moved closer, I saw her right hand clench into a fist as if about to strike. I moved no more.

"Hello," I said a second time, keeping where I was. I wanted to be as open as I could.

"Hello," she returned at last, observing me with care.

"My name is Peter York," I greeted her. "I'm from the Pennsylvania side. Are you looking to get across?"

"And if I were?" she returned with a suspicious tone that I saw no reason for her to take.

"Because the water here is too high to ford," I informed her, letting her understand that *I* was knowing. "You can't walk it, save in August or after a long dry spell. Even then you'd be too small. Do you live hereabouts?"

"Yes," she said simply.

"Where?"

"Not far," she answered. "If you live over there," she wanted to know, "what are you doing here?"

The more I looked at her, the more puzzled I became. Her clothes, which I had earlier noticed were torn, were more ragged than I had seen. And despite her fearlessly clenched fist, she did not appear strong. Her arms were too thin. And while at first glance I had thought her younger than myself, on further looking I thought she might be older, only smaller in stature than I am.

"What are you doing here?" she repeated, not for a moment unclenching her hand.

I moved to the river's edge. "Trying to get back there," I replied, pointing at Morgan's Rock.

"Is that where you live?"

"Hereabouts, three miles down," I said, not wishing to explain too much of my misadventures.

She was watching me suspiciously. "How did you get across in the first place?" she wanted to know. "By ferry?"

"No," I admitted reluctantly. "By boat."

"Where is your boat?" she demanded, seeing I was unsure in my reply.

"It broke up," I answered airily, trying to make it sound as if it were the most ordinary thing to have happened. Then, quickly, I tried to change the subject. "You haven't told me your name," I reminded her.

"Betsy," she said forthrightly.

"Betsy what?"

"Betsy Williams."

"I don't know the name," I told her. "Just where are you from?"

"Pennington."

"Where's that?"

"Above Trenton."

"That's farther than I know," I admitted.

"I hadn't money to cross by ferry," she volunteered. "I thought I could find a way of getting across on my own up here."

"Why are you crossing?" I asked.

"I've family in Doylestown. I was going there," she said.

"Alone?"

"I'm a servant girl," she told me. "But my father has become ill, so my mother sent for me and I was given leave to go," she took care to say. "There was no way to travel other than on foot."

What she said made sense to me. I knew well there

were many people poor enough not to have the coins needed to cross on the ferry. And the distance from Trenton was not so great that she could not reach Doylestown in two days' walk.

"How do you plan to cross?" she asked me. "Is this the narrowest part?"

"That's only an island," I told her, pointing toward the rock. "It's rough on this side, but on the other side it's calm. This is the worst of it. Of course," I said, showing her my knowledge, "it's high after all this rain."

"Will it get higher?" she asked. I could hear discouragement in her voice.

I shrugged. "I can't tell. But there are times it gets no higher. Mister Shinn says it's spring flood."

"Is this Mister Shinn with you?" she wanted to know.

"No," I told her, still not willing to give particulars of all the things I'd done. "He's gone off. Did you hear all those shots some time ago?"

"What about them?" she asked, looking off toward the river where I had pointed.

"That was a signal," I explained. "They're looking for some men. Runaway felons. Mister Shinn is the Justice of the Peace. But we all help in the search, to get some of the reward."

She turned from me again and looked downriver as if to study the place where the shots had been. "Do you think they caught them?" she asked nervously.

"You don't have to worry," I told her. "I'm sure they have. They wouldn't have done all that gunning unless they had. It might have been the men they were looking for who did the shooting, but I doubt it. Usually they don't have guns. It goes worse with them if they stole things when they left."

She nodded to what I had to say.

"But look here," I said, bringing her mind back to what I considered more important. "I've thought of a way to get across, but it would take two of us. Would you want to try? It'll give you a proper soaking."

"What's your way?" she inquired.

"You can't swim, can you?" I asked.

"How do you know?"

"I watched you wade into the water. It didn't look to me as if you could."

"No, I can't," she confessed.

"Well, I can," I told her. "But I wouldn't try it in this water. Not today. What I thought to do is go farther up, find a log, and ride it down to the other side of Morgan's Rock. If we go high enough, there won't be problems in slanting the log across. Do you think you want to try?"

"Your boat's truly gone?" she asked again.

"Smashed to nothing," I said with something of a brag. "Look here," I added, deciding I had to trust her. "You have to get across, and so do I. I hurt my arm when I came across before, so I'm not certain I can ride the log alone. But if we went together it would work. I'm certain it would."

She looked at me thoughtfully, as if she were searching for some secret meaning in what I said. Then she turned back to the river. "Do you really think we can?" she asked nervously.

Her obvious fear served to make me bolder. "It's easier than going to the ferry," I boasted. "Besides, you've got no money, and I'd rather go this way."

"Is anyone waiting for you on the other side?" she asked.

"No one," I said, growing impatient.

She studied me anew. "Very well," she finally said. "If you can find the log."

"We'd better go farther upstream," I told her. "At least half a mile. The farther we go, the better chance we have of not missing the island when we come down."

"I'll follow," she said.

I nodded and began to make my way north again some paces in front of her. I went slower than I might otherwise have done, for she had no shoes. All the same, she made it her brisk business not to lag behind.

So we proceeded, and I for one felt myself all but home.

4

As I reckoned it, it must have been ten in the morning when we started up the river. My hunger had increased. I was even more anxious to get back to the island, recover the gun, and return home before Mr. Shinn came to look for me, as I knew he was sure to if he returned first. I therefore put aside my hunger and hurried on as fast as I could.

Unfortunately it wasn't always possible to go fast. The girl, though she followed as well as she could, constantly lagged behind, and I had to wait for her. Not that she uttered a word of complaint. It was clear to me that she wasn't strong, and not at all used to what I was asking her to do. I might have thought more about her lack of strength, but didn't.

Nonetheless, it wasn't long before Morgan's Rock was at our backs. The sun continued to grow warmer, and a clear blue sky made me feel even cheerful, though from time to time my arm gave a twinge of pain.

The truth was I had begun to feel good again, forgetting all the shame of my follies. I even began to see what I was doing as something of an adventure, going so far as to look forward to recounting it all in the most heroic terms possible.

After we had gone on for a while, the girl called to me. "Can we rest a bit?" she asked.

I did not reply, but to show my manhood stood my ground upstream of her, graciously allowing her to sit and take her rest.

"Do you have brothers and sisters?" I asked.

"None," she replied.

"What does your father do?" I wanted to know.

"He hires out his labor," was all she replied.

Here I began to feel sorry for her. Her father was a laborer, and without land. That meant he was poor indeed, which explained why she had been put to service. Then, too, she kept her right hand folded in her lap. I wondered if she had done some injury to it, or if it was, perhaps, deformed.

"When was the last time you ate?" I asked.

She did not answer, but looked down the river again, as she would do from time to time.

"You can come to my home and stop for a while," I offered. "Mistress Shinn will be glad to help."

To this she answered nothing, and in a moment stood up. "We should go on," she said.

Once again I took up our march, in and out among the trees ranged near the river, staying as close to the water's edge as possible.

In that place the river was fairly straight so that I was able to make a decent judgment as to how far we had come above the island. When I determined we had gone about half a mile, I decided we should stop.

The brightness of the day and the ever growing warmth seemed to have no effect upon the river. The place where we stood was not broken with rapids or white water, but the river raced along at a constant speed. It had not yet begun to go down.

"There," I said. "You can see how quickly it's running. All we need do is find a log big enough to carry us. From here we'll be able to cut across with ease and come behind the island. It's safe enough," I added, seeing from her face that she was not so sure.

"There are falls farther down," she said. "I saw them."

"Two," I added. "The one below the ferry is the worst. The one up here is not so bad. We'll be safer here."

"What if we miss the island?" she asked anxiously.

"We won't," I reassured her. "We won't be any-where near the falls. I managed with my broken boat and sore arm. The two of us should do much better."

The first thing we had to do was find a log or even a broken tree big enough to support the two of us. "We'd best move higher to find what we need," I told her.

As before, the girl agreed without words and let me lead the way. I rather liked her for doing so.

It proved difficult to find what we wanted. With

no ax, it was a question of finding something on the ground big enough for us to carry, but not so big that we could not move it. After some diligent searching, we found what we needed thirty yards inland— a big old birch tree, rotten at its roots, which had partially fallen and was leaning against another tree.

"There's the one we'll take," I told her. "We can pull it down."

She came to the tree willingly enough and placed her arms around it and began to pull with me. I leaped as high as I could, grabbed the tree, and hung my weight from it. In moments we had the tree down.

It was not a tall tree, but it had many branches and was without leaves. The gray-white bark was rotten in places and pulled off easily. In size, though, it was more than four hands around.

"Shall we pull the branches off?" she asked.

I considered. "We'll need them to pull it to the river and hold on to when we cross. We'd best take it as it is."

This proved to be the best thing to have done. Both of us pulling on the branches made it easier to drag the tree to the water.

From time to time I watched her work, with particular attention to her hand. I noticed that when she used it, she seemed able to work with it fully. This convinced me that she was not deformed.

After some time, we rolled the tree into the water, but it sat so low that my entire plan seemed something less than fine. The girl looked askance at it too, and I wondered if she would refuse to go with me.

"Do you really think it will do?" she asked at last.

"As good as not," I replied with more authority than I felt. "We'd best go," I said.

So saying, I pushed the tree farther into the water, waded out into and against the current till I stood up to my middle. She remained on the shore, however, reluctant to follow.

"Are you coming?" I called, looking back.

Still she hesitated.

"Frightened?" I taunted.

At that moment we heard three distinct gunshots from the south.

"There!" I cried. "I thought they had them!"

"What do you mean?" she asked, speaking so low it was difficult, against the wash of the water, for me to hear her.

"I thought they had already caught them. They must still be at it. Perhaps they are putting up a fight." It made me want to hurry even more. "Are you coming?" I demanded. "Yes or no?"

Once more she looked downriver, and as if only then making up her mind, waded into the water after me, her skirt billowing. The water made her shiver.

"Stay on the same side as me," I called. "That will keep the tree against us. But go in front so I can make sure you do things right."

She did as I told her, passing me by.

"Now," I called, "put your arm around the trunk as I've done."

Squatting in the water, I put my right arm around the tree.

Looking back, she did the same.

"Now," I cried, "we'll push ourselves out!"

Together we began to make our way into the central current. "Draw up your feet!" I shouted.

The next moment we were afloat; the river had caught us and already our speed had increased.

5

Coming across the first time had not been difficult. The second time was not the same. I was *in* the water, not on it. And the sound was greater, overwhelming me, roaring so loudly that I had to shout to make myself heard.

Even before we could take breath, the river swung us down, our speed increasing with every passing second. That sudden, so swift movement seemed to render us senseless, for at first neither of us did a thing. I could see her before me clearly, and she, like me, did nothing more than cling to the tree.

Recovering first, I looked up and saw that we were rushing much faster downriver than I thought possible. It meant that though we had gone some half mile above Morgan's Rock, we had not gone far enough.

"Stroke the water!" I cried out. By this I meant she should paddle with her free arm, as I had begun to do, and so push us across. But she failed at first to understand and only turned a white, terrified face on me.

"Watch me!" I shouted. Holding to the tree with my right arm, I stroked madly with my left. It was yet another of my follies, for every movement I made brought on a stroke of pain.

But seeing what I was doing she at last understood and began to do the same. With the two of us paddling we began to move in the direction we wanted, actually sliding toward the river's center. Even so, our movement was far greater down the river than across it. The question clearly was, could we cut a sharp enough angle across and strike the island, or would we be swept much farther?

"Pull deeper!" I called to her, by which I meant that we had to do more than paddle on the water's surface if we were to pull ourselves in the desired direction.

This we did. More and more we began to edge toward the center. But even as that began to happen, we discovered that the river's current was not the same everywhere. At one spot it ran slowly, at another, fast. This made our crossing movement a clumsy, jerky journey. We would be pulled downriver at the fast places, only to go across quickly under our own power at quieter spots. It was for just that reason that we came into our worst troubles.

We were paddling furiously in the midst of one of the heavy, rolling sections when we suddenly lapped upon a quiet spot. Because our paddling was so strong, we bore the front of the tree completely about, directly *up* into the current. That is to say, we began to turn. The worst resulted. We found ourselves spun about. Hardly before we understood what had happened we found our positions reversed. We were heading back the way we had come, toward the *Jersey* shore!

Here again we lost important moments trying to determine what to do.

"Push back against the water," I cried above the river, starting to do so myself. The girl did the same. The results were even worse; we began to revolve in complete circles, end over end, now facing one way, now another. Frightened, dizzy, it was all we could do to hold on.

"Wait till we're pointed right," I shouted at her. "Then kick as well as paddle."

She looked at me with an awful expression, the fear of death on her face. No doubt I looked the same.

Round about we swung in a slow, graceful arc. In the pause I lifted my head and looked downriver. Morgan's Rock seemed to be rushing toward us at a speed I had not thought possible. Unless we acted quickly we would miss the island entirely and plunge over Finger Falls.

There were but a few moments given us.

"Try again, *now*," I shouted at her when we were pointed right. At once we kicked and swung our arms, making (so it seemed to me) more froth and splash than the river itself. But the spinning ceased and once again we began to make progress across in the proper way.

"I've no more strength," she called out.

"We're almost there," I returned. "We can reach it."

To my plea she responded with more effort, but each time I saw it was less and less.

Down and down we floated, making little motion across the river at all.

"More," I pleaded. "*More!*"

Somehow, she and I managed to find the strength. Kicking and swinging our arms, we began again to make headway, though my arm felt numb from pain.

Larger and larger grew the island, until I saw the rock itself—like some enormous thing. As low as I was I could see the river fling itself in high, furious foam against that solid mass.

I managed to raise my head to see where we were placed, trying to see if we could slip into the channel on the island's other side. That, I saw, was hopeless. Could we then strike the island somewhere, any-where, along its length? Of even that I was no longer sure. We had to try for whatever spot we could.

"Harder, harder," I screamed at her.

She must have sensed what I had seen, for her ef-forts became truly frantic.

How we maneuvered I cannot say. It seemed as if we were as much under the water as on it, the tree tipping and spinning now this way, now that. At one point the place to which I held broke way, so I had to snatch a branch with my other hand.

"I can't do any more," she cried. And, indeed, her struggle, as well as mine, seemed without effect.

"Hold on," I shouted. "Don't let go."

In desperation she turned herself about, flinging her other arm over the tree and resting her head there, her hair drawn through the water. Hanging on, no more and no less, she gave herself up to being carried.

I still tried to paddle.

The island's rock was not twenty yards down-stream of us. Whatever strength remained in me I spent pushing, swinging. It was useless. We slid down the river faster and faster yet again.

The worst then came upon us. We were sucked into the swirling eddies, which pulled us around the rock itself. Before, the river's water had seem to fly. Now it turned upon itself with no beginning and no end.

All effort was meaningless. We shot down those last few feet faster than ever. The roar of the white-foamed water was everywhere. I felt myself pushed and pulled as the face of the rock rose up above like some living thing intent upon destroying us. With a tremendous jolt, we were thrown up against Morgan's Rock.

6

The water, now at its most hateful, hammered us unmercifully. The sound was equal to its force, a constant roar, as though the whole bloated river had gathered one tongue to make one violent note and that one note screamed in our ears.

The tree to which we clung must have gotten wedged into a high crevice in the rock, for it stuck out like a quivering lance. To this lance we clung, dangling, unable to move.

I tried to call out to her, but for my effort received only water enough to choke. But I could see her through the foam. She was hanging from the tree, frantically struggling to find a place of safety. Her predicament was worse than mine, however, for her skirt pulled her about, making her dance like a doll at the end of a string.

Still holding to the tree, I tried to move toward her—she being closer to the rock than I—so as to shield her from the water's force. But the branches prevented me from making any meaningful movement. Something in my effort must have unhinged the tree, however, for with a ponderous lurch it shifted downward, though it did not free itself of the rock. Hanging lower, I turned to reassure her, but could no longer see her.

Twisting, I looked down and realized that she had slipped past me. Now she was lower on the tree than I was, still holding to a branch. This was so even as she was pulled around the far edge of the rock. I leaned down, attempting to reach her, but the tree's branches prevented it. Then I saw her grip give way. Such was the force of the water, and such was her light weight, that for a moment she was held in the air, pinned to one spot. She hung there, desperately attempting to find a place to hold.

The tree, relieved of her weight, began to shift again. My own grasp gave way. Losing my hold, I flung my hands toward her and touched her arm, taking it in an embrace of desperation. Down we plunged into the green-white and wild waters. It was as though my soul were being taken from me.

Withal, by some sure grace of God, we managed to cling together. And the water, as if compelled to admit defeat, fairly tossed us around the rock's edge, flinging us down its side. On that instant the great pounding gave way to what, by contrast, seemed a perfect calm.

We floated together, I making frantic efforts, she but the feeblest of moves. I strove by kicking—I had long since lost my boots—to bring us closer to the island. There the river, further repentant of all it had done, actually helped us, pushing us as before but edging us toward the shore. At last I felt the sublime touch of ground beneath my feet. This sense of something solid gave me strength. I pulled once again and found that I could stand. We were not to drown. Oh, thee who always walk the earth and know not the blessed ground!

I tried to push her off, but neither of us had the strength to stand alone. We hung one upon the other for such strength as we could muster. In such a manner we waded to the shore, where we threw ourselves down on the dry land. At once she rolled away and began to vomit great quantities of water.

When her purging had ceased, she picked herself up, and though exhausted, moved up higher to a tree. Here she sat, her head hanging limply, her eyes closed.

For myself, I simply sat on the shore, too sore to move or speak, my eyes seeing but dimly.

It was I who regained strength first. Getting up, I went to her side and knelt beside her to see if I could be of help.

Sensing my presence, she half opened her eyes, but whether she truly saw me I could not tell, for they closed again quickly. Feeling I could help, I took her left hand and began to rub it for warmth. I then turned to her right hand and began to rub that between my hands.

It was then I saw it, saw it instantly. She had a brand on her thumb.

The brand was *M*-shaped, reddish brown, unmistakably a burn, distinct, clearly placed, and clearly meant to be seen. *M*, for malefactor. It meant she was a felon, one of those for whom we had hunted.

I sat facing her, trying to calm myself. Instead, as if suddenly mindful of my own condition, I began to shiver, feeling a great chill upon my body. My arm ached, too. I felt exhausted in every sense I knew.

Nonetheless, for a long time we sat that way, neither of us moving, my eyes fixed on her, though she, I think, slept. I only stared, content at first to let the river sounds be at one with the tumult in my head. I knew not what to do.

PART THREE

The Promise

1

Despite my desire to turn away, I kept looking at her hand, the one that bore the brand. Even in her sleep she had it curled into a fist, no doubt from force of habit. More than once I was tempted to lean forward and pry her fingers open to look at it again. But I was afraid to do it.

So we sat, not moving, she asleep and I trying to decide how best to act.

As I thought about who she was and what she had been, I began to put aside our crossing of the river, put it aside as of no account. Instead, I saw her only as the runaway we had sought, the felon we had looked for. I—*I alone*—had caught her.

The longer I sat there, the more that sense of triumph grew, unfurling gaudy images within my mind of my return home. I saw myself bringing the girl to Mr. Shinn's house, claiming the reward for her capture, a great victory that would wipe away my other failings. The more I thought of it, the more it pleased me and the more I knew what I wanted to do. So it was that I decided to pretend to have noticed nothing and find a way to get her to return home with me.

In time she opened her eyes. I felt compelled to make idle chatter, lest she suspect what I had decided.

"We didn't go up the river enough," I said. "It was my fault what happened."

"Are we in Pennsylvania?" she asked.

"We're on the island," I explained. "There's only the channel to go. You won't have any trouble with that."

"I thought we weren't going to reach it at all," she said.

"Aye, but I set you to it," I replied. "I suppose I had to get you out."

She leaned her head against the tree again, lapsing into silence.

"My home's not far away," I blurted out. "You could come back with me. There's someone there—Mistress Shinn—she'll mend your clothing."

She opened her eyes and looked intently at me. Uncomfortable under her gaze, I turned away, beginning to worry that she might guess what I was about. "You would not believe all the foolish things I've done today," I said, feeling the need to say something.

She didn't respond.

"You see," I continued, almost afraid to stop, "Mister Shinn and I went hunting last night. That's how I came to sprain my arm. I tripped on something and fell. Then, when we had to go, I remembered I'd left my gun on this island."

"What were you hunting?" she asked.

"Rabbits," I said, coming to my feet. "But he lost patience with me and left. I had to come back alone. That was on the boat. That's when I was carried to the Jersey shore. I told you about that."

She started to get up.

"We don't have to go yet," I urged, all but pushing her back down. "You can rest for a while more. I'll fetch the gun and come back. It won't take long. Then we'll go."

Her eyes still on me, I paused before I went, uncertain. Then, remembering my decision, I left quickly, keeping to the island's shore.

I went hastily, though easily enough, considering that I was without my boots. I found the spot where Mr. Shinn and I had kept watch the night before. From there I could find the place where I had put the gun. It was just where I had left it. Even Mr. Shinn's handkerchief was there.

Stuffing the linen cloth into my pocket, I reloaded the gun, priming it carefully, though my fingers trembled. I wanted to be sure I had it ready to use.

Gun in hand, my heart beating with nervousness, I returned the way I'd come along the shore. But when I reached the spot where I had left her, she was gone.

2

That the girl was gone confounded me. For a few moments I could do nothing but stand there gaping. I had left her weak enough, or so it seemed, that the thought of her going anywhere had not even remotely occurred to me.

I was so startled that my reaction was one of anger, anger that she should have betrayed me. I who had saved her. I who had trusted her!

With such sentiments bursting in upon me, it's hardly a surprise what I did next. I plunged into the thicket in pursuit, assuming that she was trying to escape and was making for the narrow channel I had told her about.

Pushing my way through the heavy growth proved no easier than it had earlier. The tangled mass of trees and bushes caught me with every hasty, rushing step. My bare feet were no help. More than once I tripped and had to catch myself from falling. Nonetheless I plunged on, straight across what I thought would be the fastest way to the island's other side.

As I fought my way through, I became angrier. She was in the wrong to run away from me. It made me all the more determined to make her my prisoner. I would show her—I would show everyone—that I was not to be trifled with.

Out I burst on the Pennsylvania side of the island, there to stand upon the shore. But looking up and down I saw nothing, not one clue to indicate where she was.

My perplexity was great. For if she didn't come that way, she could only be hiding on the island. The area in which she could conceal herself was small, but within it she could be anywhere. And, I must confess it, I even considered that she might attack me.

I thought of firing my gun to signal the other men, who might still be on the hunt. I checked myself, however, when I considered how they would mock me for my inability to catch her. How could I not catch her? I asked myself. Wasn't she only a girl? Not to catch her by myself would be the greatest dishonor of all.

Once more I checked the priming of my rifle, making sure it would not misfire. That done, I turned toward the island.

I decided I'd be best served if I stayed on the western side of the island, reasoning that she was intent on reaching the mainland and thus would have to pass me at some point. Further, I assumed that she would never again cast herself into the main current of the river. In that sense I had her trapped on Morgan's Rock.

I took my first stand at the spot where I commanded the widest possible view, hoping to cut her off the moment she revealed herself.

Just how long I waited I'm not sure. It could not have been more than moments, for I was impatient, nervous, and impulsive. I preferred to move about.

Wading farther into the water, I slowly stepped northward up the channel, toward the rock itself. My gun was in readiness, its flint cocked. I moved cautiously, as silently as possible, casting looks forward and behind. Even so, the splashing of my steps seemed loud. I forced myself to walk slower.

Gradually I moved upstream until I could get no closer to the rock without being in the water about its base. There the vegetation was sparse. I could see across the whole island.

She was not there.

Turning about, I started back downstream covering the same area I had gone over before, but moving with yet more care, peering into the tree cover and bushes as I went.

Still she eluded me.

With every moment my frustration mounted. I made myself continue south, stopping, turning with each step, my rifle always ready.

When I had crossed perhaps one-quarter down the island's length, she sprang out some twenty feet behind me like the bursting of a pheasant from the bush.

I must have passed right in front of her without noticing her at all. Now she leaped frantically into the water, and abandoning all pretense of concealing herself, plunged into the channel, skipping this way and that, trying to reach the mainland.

As soon as I had recovered from my surprise, I shouted, "Stop!"

She paid me no heed, but continued to run.

I lifted my rifle to my shoulder even as I called my warning once again.

But she listened to me no more than she had done before.

I aimed and pulled the trigger. The rifle fired. Her high, sharp cry upon being hit was instantaneous. Halfway around she spun, then collapsed into the water as if dead.

When I saw what I had done I stood there motionless, horrified. I was certain that I had killed her. It was as if the Lord's fist had reached down and gripped me around the chest, squeezing out every breath I had.

How long I stood there I cannot say, but it was long enough for me to fling the gun away as if it were some defiled thing. Where it went I never knew, for I never saw it again.

I ran forward to where she lay in water already red

with blood and hauled her up. She made no resistance. Frantically, I dragged her back toward the island, unmindful of any hurt I might be doing.

At the shore I lay her on the ground, face up. Her eyes were closed, her face a dreadful white, her soaking hair marked with red. I forced myself to search for where I had struck her. It was not difficult to find, for the blood still flowed. The bullet had cut her arm. No more, but no less either.

A sensation of joy that the wound was no worse swept over me, to be immediately followed by a renewed fear for what I had done. Hastily I pulled Mr. Shinn's handkerchief from my pocket and tried to stop the blood. But the linen cloth was too small.

I pulled off my shirt and, trembling, began to tear at it, trying to create long strips. These I tightly bound around her wound to stop the blood. It worked better than the handkerchief had done; the bleeding lessened.

Stepping back, I saw that the ground on which she lay was wet and marshy. I had to move her. When I picked her up, she moaned. What her cry when I had shot her had not done, what her blood had not done, that one sound accomplished. I began to cry, great sobbing cries that shook me. I was crying for her, and for myself, tears I had not allowed myself when I was most alone. Even so, I carried her inland, trying to find a place to put her.

I stumbled about, all but falling, till I found a place. Then I eased her down, leaning her against a tree.

Checking the strips I had tied around her arm, I saw to my relief that the bleeding had abated. I tied the knots tighter, then stood back to watch.

She opened her eyes, but seemed completely numb, unable to say a thing.

I had never before been so frightened. I was afraid to move, yet afraid not to, for I did not know how dangerous her condition was. I believed—I wanted to believe—that the wound was slight. But still I couldn't choose whether to stay with her or go for help. Either way might prove fatal. As it was, I did nothing, but remained standing before her with the vague hope that my wishes and my prayers—which I offered up in multitudes through my tears—would be of help to her, as well as to me.

When at last she opened her eyes fully, it was only to stare at me.

"Forgive me," I stammered clumsily. "I didn't think to hurt you. I didn't."

She gave no reply.

Not knowing what else to do, I sat down before her and waited. In time she asked for water, which I was only too glad to bring her in my hands. Having sucked it up, she managed to hold up her head and keep her eyes open, though she continued to look only at me.

That look kept me there until she lifted her right arm, extended her palm, and put the branded hand in front of my eyes.

"Forgive me," I repeated, unable to look.

Her hand dropped. Her eyes closed. She gave me no reply.

"Does it hurt very much?" I ventured after a while.

She would not say.

"Do you want me to get help?" I tried.

Still she made no reply.

"I could take you to my home," I pleaded. "Mistress Shinn will help you. I know she will."

She shook her head, no.

"I promise," I fairly pleaded. "You won't be harmed." I went on to give her every reason I could think of why she should allow me to bring her there.

To none of these would she agree, but kept shaking her head obstinately to everything I said.

Then, in the midst of all my urging, we heard a voice.

"Peter! Peter York! Are thee there?"

Mr. Shinn had come back to find me.

3

The sound of his voice—he was standing on the mainland—was enough to transform us both. The defiance she'd made bold to show evaporated to nothing. In its place, clearly, stood nothing but fear. Willing enough to contradict me, only a boy and her equal, to face the world beyond was another thing.

I myself feared what Mr. Shinn would do.

Again his voice came, more insistent now, so I knew he was worried that I had not replied. I stood up, but didn't know what to do.

"Don't tell them I'm here," she whispered urgently. "Tell them you never saw me. Don't give me to them."

"Peter!" came Mr. Shinn's voice, loud, clear, and with even greater urgency.

I made up my mind. "I won't tell them," I told her. "But you mustn't leave. Stay here. Will you promise?"

"I can't," she answered. "They'll find me."

"They won't," I insisted. "I'll come back as soon as I can, with food. You mustn't try to go alone. Give me your word," I asked. "Believe me, I won't tell them. I'll help you get away. I promise!"

Unable to wait any longer for her answer, I shouted

back to Mr. Shinn. "I'm here!" I turned to the girl again. "I'll come back as soon as I can," I told her. "I'll come," I repeated. "I will."

Not daring to take any more time, I left, leaping through the trees and undergrowth. "I'm coming," I called to Mr. Shinn, hurrying lest he come on the island.

I went down to the island's shore, shouting every step along the way, trying to make as much noise as possible so as to assure him that I was, in fact, coming. In moments I broke through. Mr. Shinn was standing on the landing. Jumper was with him.

His reaction when he saw me was one of astonishment. "Peter!" he cried, his questions tumbling out. "Where's thy clothing, thy boots? What's happened to the boat? Have thee lost the rifle?"

In my eagerness to show myself I had completely forgotten the way I looked.

"What have thee done?" he demanded.

"I've been very stupid," I replied. "The boat's gone. So is the gun."

"That boat was not ours," he said severely. Then he recalled something else. "But I heard gunshot," he said. "Was it not thee who fired?"

That, too, I had forgotten. "No," I lied. "It wasn't."

"It startled us," he said. "We had hoped it was thee."

"Didn't you catch them?" I asked.

"Only one," he said. "The other is still missing."

Suddenly impatient, he told me to come across. I moved at once into the channel.

"Be careful," he called out. "The water is still high."

I went easily enough, walking all the way, though at one point I had to stand on tiptoe. After what I had passed over, the current there was as nothing to me.

"It's no longer rising," he informed me. "And a good thing, too, or thee couldn't walk it."

When I was close enough, he held out his hand and in seconds I stood on the shore. There he scrutinized me.

"Thee have nothing but rags," he said, shaking his head in puzzlement. He took off his jacket and put it around me. Then he mounted Jumper and pulled me up behind him, unmindful of my wetness.

"Now tell me what thee has done," he commanded as we started on. "Tell it all. I need to know."

Glad enough to leave the place, I told him all I could as we rode along. I started from the first: where I had placed the rifle, how I had twisted my arm, how in seeking to retrieve the gun I had mismanaged the boat because of my sprained arm, and how I had cut across the river.

"Thee should have just jumped off the boat," he said when I told him that part.

I related how I had come back across the second time; that I had gone upriver, found a tree, and rode it back down to the island. I told him how I'd been thrown up against Morgan's Rock and how narrowly I had escaped drowning.

To that he said: "God looked upon thee there."

In short I told him everything that happened with all the detail and truthfulness I could—save one enormous fact. I mentioned absolutely nothing of the girl.

"Why did thee not just walk to Coryell's Ferry?" he wanted to know. I could tell that he was upset, though he tried not to show it.

"I was ashamed to admit what I'd done," I replied.

"That was the worst foolishness of all!" he said with a sharpness that made me jump.

"I know," I said simply.

Once I had related all that happened we went along in silence, though I knew he was carefully thinking over what I had said.

"When did thee lose the gun?" he broke the silence to ask.

"When I crossed the first time," I answered too quickly. "When the boat smashed on the Jersey side."

"Ah," he said. "I thought thee said it was while going to *get* the gun that thee were swept away."

Afraid that he would catch me in another mistake,

I dared not say a word. He gave me no reason to suspect that he was anything but satisfied with my reply, however, for he asked no further questions. We continued on in silence.

"What about the bondsman you caught?" I asked him after a while.

"Thee will see him soon enough," he said. "He's being held prisoner at the house."

4

We rode back to the farm, I all the while wishing that we had another horse. Not for the old reasons, but because of a desire to be alone. I had made my decision to free the girl so quickly that I felt unsure what I might say. We talked no more.

When we got home I jumped down immediately and went toward the door. Mistress Shinn came out to greet us. As soon as she saw my condition she grew alarmed and wanted to be of help.

I wanted no comfort, however. I passed her by, pausing only long enough to see that Mr. Shinn was telling all she wanted to know. In any case, she inquired no further of me, but seemed to know what had occurred.

The children greeted me with a mixture of astonishment and hooted remarks at my ragged condition. I took it all without rejoinder, neither willing nor in truth able to share my thoughts with them.

I changed out of my filthy britches into dry garments, putting on an old pair of boots which, though tight, were suitable enough. I was in no mood to complain. Even my arm felt somewhat better.

As I came down from the loft I found that Mistress Shinn had laid out food for me. She had set down cornbread, molasses, meat, and cider. Ravenous, I could hardly eat enough.

I thought of hiding away some food for the girl, but realized it was not worth the risk. I knew where the food was kept, and had access to it whenever I might be hungry. I decided to wait till later.

When I completed my meal, Mistress Shinn informed me that her husband was waiting for me. I went outside at once.

"Would thee like to see the bondsman we caught?" he asked.

I was not at all certain that I wanted to, but my curiosity was too strong. I let him lead me. As we went, he told me of the capture.

The prisoner had apparently managed to get across the river, just how they did not know, but perhaps hidden on a cart that was carried on the ferry. In any case, Issac Waterford had seen him coming up along the banks of the river. It then became a question of surrounding him. But the prisoner proved to be too artful. That was why Waterford had requested help. It had not been easy, but they had at last cornered the bondsman. It was Mr. Shinn who had convinced him that he had no choice but to surrender.

Mr. Shinn related all this to me as we made our way to the small wooden outbuilding where he kept his tools. I saw that those things had been removed. The door, too, which was usually closed with nothing more than a stick, now had an iron bar in its clasp.

"How old is the prisoner?" I asked suddenly.

Mr. Shinn looked at me curiously. "Why do thee ask that?"

"I don't know," I mumbled, sorry I had spoken.

He considered the question. "Thee shall see for thyself," he answered.

At the door he bade me stand back, lest the prisoner be against the door, waiting to spring out. First he called in to the person, telling him to stand clear. Only then did he pull back the door.

The prisoner was not in fact near the door, but was sitting against the farthest wall facing us when we looked in. Sure enough, as I had feared, they had caught a boy. He was even younger than the girl, no more than ten years of age. In the darkness of the place I could see that he was dirty, his clothing ill-made. Like the girl, he wore no shoes. His hair was in great disorder.

But what struck me most about him when I saw him in the dim light was the look of indifference with which he received us. He showed no anger, no fear, no reproach. It was as if a hand had flattened away all expression and left him no more than alive. How different, I thought, from the reaction of the girl.

"Who is he?" I whispered.

"He gives his name as Robert," Mr. Shinn said.

"Is he a felon?" I asked, talking before the boy as if he weren't there.

"I'm not certain," Mr. Shinn replied. "There's no brand on him. He says he isn't. Word has been sent to Trenton informing John Tolivar that we have him."

Until Mr. Shinn shut the door I continued to stare at the boy. He had not said a word all the while we stood before him. Nor, as much as I could see, had he even blinked.

We went back toward the house.

"Will you return him?" I asked.

"I must," he said.

To this I said nothing, and we continued on. But something in *my* silence seemed to irk him.

"It's as I told thee this morning," he said impatiently. "It's not for me to say this law, that law. I'm bound to uphold all laws. Can thee understand that?"

"Yes, sir," I replied, not wishing to argue with him. He seemed satisfied.

But as we came to the house I asked him one other thing. "How long will he remain here?"

"I told thee," he said impatiently. "I've sent word to Trenton. I assume he'll be sent for. It will be no more than a day or two." So saying, he went inside the house. I preferred to remain outside.

I did not stay there long. To my surprise, Mr. Shinn called the family together, informing us that we were in need of special prayer. This was most unusual, for though they were a prayerful family I had not known him to do that before. Clearly, something was troubling Mr. Shinn, and the meeting was meant to help him find his way.

Accordingly we gathered as at regular Quaker meeting. Mistress Shinn with her daughters sat to one side of the room, I and their son sat opposite. Mr. Shinn, as elder, sat between, up front.

When we were settled, he bowed his head. As was the Quaker custom, we sat in silence waiting for God's inner light—as they expressed it—to move us to speak. All, young and old, were free to do so.

I, too, bowed my head.

Shortly after we began, Mr. Shinn looked up and spoke. "Our friend Peter York," he said, "has come close to death today. It behooves us, and him, to think upon it." He said no more, and all heads bowed again.

I thought not of death but about the girl. I knew I had an obligation to speak out. It was not just the lies I had told, but what I hoped to do for her. Glancing up, I found Mr. Shinn's eyes on me. I tried to meet them, but couldn't. I bowed my head again. Once or twice I was certain he would speak. In the end he was not so moved, and the meeting closed as silently as it began.

When he concluded the meeting, I asked permission to rest, for I was greatly worn. This was granted easily enough, with cautions to the younger ones to leave me at peace.

I lay on my bed in the loft. Though I was very tired—I had hardly slept the night before—I could not sleep. Visions of the shooting kept repeating in my mind. Each time, I was shamed anew.

I thought, too, about the boy in the outbuilding and how he had looked.

Most of all, I wondered about Mr. Shinn. What did he suspect?

Increasingly I reminded myself of the promise I had made to the girl: I would help her get free. That I felt I had to do. But now the question of the other prisoner made its way into my mind. How could I free the girl and not the boy? I asked myself. And if I freed him as well, would I not be twice at fault, twice in blame? And what would be the consequence?

More than once I wanted to get up and lay the truth before Mr. Shinn. I was too fearful, however, of what he might do. Had he not said he *must* uphold the law? He had—he had.

So I lay, my head awhirl. In time, even that was little match for my exhaustion and I slipped into troubled, restless sleep.

5

I must have slept for only about three hours, for when I awoke the day was still bright. Alarmed that I had slept too long, I scrambled down from the loft and found Mistress Shinn at work. I also found the captured boy sitting at the table, eating. To my wondering look Mistress Shinn informed me that she had decided the boy would stay in the house during the day. Only at night would he return to the shed.

While she made this explanation the boy did not so much as consider me, but continued with his food.

I requested something to eat for myself, telling her that I was very hungry. She gave me an extra large piece of bread and some cheese. "I'll eat outside," I told her. My remark made the boy look up. He thought, I'm sure, that I went because I did not wish to eat with him.

At the door I paused. "Where is Mister Shinn?" I asked.

"He went to town," she said, "to find the man who owned the boat. He says thee are forgiven thy work today."

Grateful for the easy freedom, I bolted through the door only to have the young children surround me. Having had no time to ask questions earlier, they promptly demanded knowledge of all I had done. At other times I might have regaled them with my tale. This time I went briskly past, informing them I wanted to walk alone. One girl made a show of following me, but I chased her away.

I started off in one direction as if to examine my clean britches, which were drying on a fence. When I was sure that no one was watching, I veered off and, carrying the bread and cheese, hastened north along River Road.

The distance, as I have said, was about three miles, but before I had gone by horse. On foot it took much longer. It was late in the afternoon when I reached the river landing, the approach to Morgan's Rock. And there was a difficulty I had quite forgot.

If I were to act in secrecy, and that I felt the need

to do—I could not return home again all wet. It would have been hopeless to explain it away and would have required still more lies, which I wanted to avoid. With that in mind I took off my boots, britches, and shirt, rolling everything up around the food I'd brought. I then waded into the channel and walked across, holding the bundle over my head. Happily the water had begun to go down.

I reached the other side and dressed, no worse than a little damp. Then I hastened toward the place where I had left the girl. As I went, I moved noisily so as not to come upon her suddenly and cause undue fright. But such precautions proved in vain; when I reached the spot, I found her fast asleep. No footfall would have broken into that sleep.

I shook her foot and she woke instantly, alarmed. But when she saw it was me, she gave me something of a smile, which broadened when I produced the food.

I asked her about her arm. She informed me that it was somewhat sore, although she was well enough. In any case she was far more interested in what I had brought, which I took to be a good omen. Indeed, she ate with such appetite it was clear I could have given her twice as much. While she ate, I plied her with my questions.

"What is your name?" I asked. "Your real name."

"Elizabeth," she returned, between mouthfuls.

"Elizabeth what?"

"Mawes."

"From what place?"

"England."

"And then from Trenton?" I prompted.

She nodded.

"You were running away."

"Yes."

"Why?" I wanted to know.

She looked at me as if she did not understand what I had asked. I felt compelled to repeat it. "Why did you run away?" I said again.

"I wanted to be free," she replied with perfect ease.

"You would have been free in time," I ventured. "It can only be worse for you if you're caught."

"I was owned until I came of age," she said. "Ten more years."

To that I had no reply. "Why were you branded?" I asked.

This she considered for a moment. "I was a thief," she said.

"Then you admit it," I said, surprised.

She looked at me as if I were a curious thing, and shrugged. "I stole a ring from a lady."

"Why?" I asked earnestly.

"A man said he would feed me if I did."

"Would no one have done that without your stealing?"

It was her turn to be surprised. "No," she said with perfect frankness. "Why should they?"

Her answers bewildered me, they were so far from my own understanding.

"Have you no father or mother?"

"My mother is in England," she answered. "My father is dead."

"Tell me what happened to you," I asked.

"I was caught taking the ring," she said, "and placed in prison. There I pleaded mercy. That way I gained the King's pardon on promise of transportation. I was then sold to a merchant who brings felons to the colonies. He brought me to Philadelphia, where I was sold for my labor till I become twenty-one years of age. A Trenton man bought me."

"And the brand?" I dared to asked.

"Done in the English court."

Unable to grasp it all, I turned to what I knew. "You ran away with someone, didn't you?"

For the first time she refused to answer. "Were you really going to Doylestown?" I tried.

"No," she admitted. "It's what we agreed to say. We were going to a place called Easton. We were told that it was far enough away so no one would look for us there. They said we could hire out our labor there."

"But it doesn't matter where you go," I said. "People will see your brand."

She shrugged again. "They say I'm young enough for it to fade."

"They'll only hunt you and make you return," I warned. "When an escaped bondsman is returned, he's whipped in every county through which he has passed. It's the law."

"You said you'd help me get away," she said.

"It's a crime to do so," I told her.

"I never asked your help," she rebuked me in sudden anger. Then, seeing she had upset me, she spoke in different tones. "What's your name?" she asked.

"Peter York."

Her thoughts seemed to drift. Suddenly she blurted out, "Have they caught my friend?"

I nodded.

"Did they hurt him?" she whispered as if afraid to ask. She watched my face carefully.

"No," I said. "They did send word to Trenton, though, to say that he's captured."

I could see she was very upset. "Where is he now?" she wanted to know.

"At my home," I told her. "He's allowed to stay in the house during the day." I wanted her to know that.

"Will you tell him I'm here?" she asked.

"If you want me to," I said.

She searched the ground, and finding a twig, picked it up and began to pull it apart. "He's not a thief, as

I was," she began. "I stole that ring from a jeweler to whom he was apprenticed. He took pity on me, and though younger than I, he tried to help me. He was the only friend I had. But they found him out and used him to track me down, then brought him to the magistrate as well as me. We were both put in prison. When we were transported, we stayed together. It was very bad where we were in Trenton. He swore he'd run away. I begged him to let me go with him." She had been looking at the ground while she talked. "Do you still mean to help me get free?"

"Aye."

"I mustn't leave him," she whispered. "Could you let him go free as well? He'd do no harm."

Hurriedly, I stood up. "I've got to go," I announced. "I'll come again as soon as possible. I'll bring more food next time."

"What about him?" she pleaded.

But I was already moving off. I didn't want to answer that question.

6

It was growing late, so I moved in haste to the river's edge and across as I had come. Once on the other side I ran most of the way back home, angry at myself for feeling jealous of the boy. I knew how wrong and mean that was.

As I came off the road and approached the house I saw Mr. Shinn leading the boy toward the outbuilding. Without allowing myself to be seen, I watched them go. The boy offered no resistance, but he walked in slow, methodical steps that Mr. Shinn did not choose to change.

Mr. Shinn led him to the shed, opened the door, and let the boy pass in. "Good night," I heard him say. Then he shut the door and made it fast. For a moment he paused, then slowly he retraced his steps toward the house.

For a long time I stood there, trying to make up my mind about the boy. Should I free him or not? Carefully I walked behind the outbuilding and placed my mouth to a crack in the wood. "Can you hear me?" I called softly.

There was no answer.

"Can you hear me?" I repeated, a little louder.

"Who is it?" the boy replied at last.

"It's me. Peter York. The boy who lives here."

"What do you want?" he asked, clearly annoyed.

"It's about Elizabeth," I said.

"Where is she?" he demanded, his voice suddenly full of emotion.

"She's safe," I continued in a whisper. "But you must not say I told you. I mean to help her get free," I added impulsively.

"And me?" he said at once. "Are you going to free me too?"

I took a breath.

"Will you?" he asked again.

It was as if I had only been wanting the question to be asked again. "If you're willing," I returned.

He didn't reply.

"Did you hear me?" I demanded.

"Do you mean it?" he wanted to know.

"Yes, of course."

I heard him scramble closer to the crack. "What do you want me to do?" he whispered excitedly, his manner suddenly trusting.

"I'm not sure," I confessed. "I'll find a way." Without saying more I bolted away, hurrying toward the house.

The family was at the table. They all looked up when I came in, but it was Mr. Shinn who concerned me most. Perhaps it was my sense of guilt, but I could not help feeling that he knew what I was about. I sat down hastily.

"Peter," Mr. Shinn said.

I looked up. "Yes, sir."

"A party is being made up tomorrow to search for the missing felon. I want thee to join them."

After dinner I spent a good deal of time with Jumper in her stall, stroking her sides, feeding her, but mostly seething with anger at what Mr. Shinn had asked me to do. His demand only served to confirm my fears that he suspected something. I was equally sure that he did not know the particulars, that sending me with the search party was his way of trying to force me to speak.

If anything resolved me to remain silent and continue with my plan it was that.

I stayed with Jumper for a long time, thinking out what I was doing. The more I thought, the more I realized that it would make my life with Mr. Shinn intolerable. After all had been discovered—and how could it not be?—he would have to cast me out of his house, if not arrest me. How could he do otherwise? Had he not said, "It's not for me to say this law, that law. I'm required to uphold all laws." He, the pious Justice of the Peace, harboring one who let runaway felons escape. The thought of what he might do to me made me livid. How I marked him for a hypocrite!

Such thoughts kept running through my mind when I went to bed. Even so, I don't know when the

idea came to grow, but as I lay there it did come—
that I would be forced to leave, forced to go away.
The more I thought about it, the more determined I
was not to allow that humiliation to occur. I would
leave before Mr. Shinn could act.

Once I made that decision, I realized how much I
always wanted to go away, to rid myself of the con-
straints under which I had been placed. It would be
easy enough, I thought. If the two runaways, a boy
and girl both younger than myself, could find their
way alone, so could I.

That was the promise I made to myself: I would
flee with them to Easton.

PART FOUR

The Roads of Night

1

I usually rose early, for I had a variety of tasks to do, including the care of Jumper. But next morning, no doubt because of my great tiredness, I awoke late. And when I did, I heard voices outside.

Scampering down the ladder from the loft, not even pausing to say good morning to Mistress Shinn, I hurried outside. Mr. Shinn was there. So, too, were a number of neighborhood men, Isaac Waterford and Robert Pall among them, so I knew it was the search party. They were waiting, I knew not for what. But greatly agitated at what might happen, I made bold to sit down by the front door and look on. No sooner had I done this than Mr. Shinn strode over.

Quickly I stood up.

"Good morning," he said to me softly. "They're waiting for word from Trenton before they start again. Are thee ready to join them?"

"I don't want to," I managed to say.

"Why not?" he demanded, his eyes studying my face. He actually seemed disappointed.

"I'm too tired," I said, trying to keep in my anger. I retreated back into the house.

Once inside, I discovered the boy was already sitting silently in a corner. In my rush to get out I had not noticed him. Now he looked up at me. Briefly, we stared at one another as if to seal our words of the night before, breaking away when Mistress Shinn, who was at the fire, turned about.

"Will thee be going with the search party, Peter?" she wanted to know.

"I'd rather not," I answered, taking a cup of milk and some bread from her hand.

"I suppose thee has had enough of searching." Her eyes questioned. She stopped her work to look at me.

"I guess I have," I murmured, sitting at the table still trying to decide how to act. "Do you know where they're bound?" I asked her after a moment.

"No, I don't," she replied. "Thee had best ask Mister Shinn."

Lifting my eyes, I again looked at the boy. He, more prudent than I, kept his eyes down.

I ate rapidly, and though I wanted to avoid Mr. Shinn, I made myself go out again, loitering about so as to learn what I could. Once more, as soon as he saw me, like some tormenter he came to my side.

"Are thee certain thee will not go?" he asked.

"I told you no," I said bitterly. "I've had enough of searching."

"I have to go," he informed me evenly. "But I'd like thee to do thy work today. Is thy arm better?"

"I think so."

"Good. I began to turn the ground in the western field. It's heavy yet. But if thee did some more, it would be a good thing."

To this I agreed, noting to myself that he had given me a task that would ensure my not leaving the farm.

As he so often did, he seemed to be wanting to say something more but decided against doing so. Instead he went to stand among the men, where he listened mutely to their talk. Very soon thereafter, a man rode up whom I recognized as the servant of John Tolivar —the man from Trenton.

Without dismounting, the man saluted those who were waiting.

"Gentlemen!" he called. "Mister Tolivar thanks you much for your assistance in this matter which is of some importance to him. He very much appreciates the fact that you've already captured one of the runaways and humbly begs you to continue your search. The other, he asked me to say, is every bit as valuable to him. He begs you to excuse his not coming. Hearing of your first success, he celebrated rather too much, and thinks that he might be of more hindrance than help."

The men laughed.

"However," continued the servant, "he hopes to come tomorrow and reclaim his own. He has asked me to inform you that if you are successful in finding the other, he will add another pound reward to the twelve pounds already pledged. Mister Tolivar begs to remain your most humble servant!"

"Very fine of the gentleman," allowed Richard Pall. "We thank him. You may tell Mister Tolivar that we will try our best to give him cause for another celebration, in the hope that we may be invited, too!"

To this the other men agreed with great alacrity.

The servant, offering a grand salute to the men, turned his horse and hastened away.

After he had gone, the men of the search party became serious again, gathering around to consider how they might proceed.

"Did the boy we've caught say where the two were parted?" someone asked Mr. Shinn.

"He did not," was the reply.

"You could beat it out of him if you had a mind," it was suggested.

"I've no such mind," returned Mr. Shinn. "But perhaps," he said in a voice loud enough for me to hear, "perhaps Peter York might have some thoughts where the other is. He's much the same age."

These words took me completely by surprise. Worse, all the men turned around to hear my reply.

"Peter," pressed Mr. Shinn. "Does thee have any sense where the other might have gone?" he asked.

Unprepared, unsure, and furious for what he was doing, I could hardly answer. "I?" I stumbled.

"Yes, thee," he said.

While I sought an answer, I could only look at the ground about my feet. I knew I must reply. Despite Mr. Shinn's cruelty, I saw it was an opportunity to send them the wrong way.

"If she could not cross by the ferry," I finally said, "perhaps she's still in Jersey. She couldn't swim the river, it's still far too strong."

Mr. Shinn looked at me so piercingly when I said this that I avoided his eyes lest mine give me away. But he demanded no more, only saying, "Perhaps the girl *is* hiding by the ferry. Most likely Coryell's. I think we should look there."

This, to my great relief, seemed to meet with general approval. The men mounted, and I watched as they moved off south. As they went, Mr. Shinn, up on Jumper, swung around to look at me. Our eyes met. Clearly he was angry at me. How I hated him then! How glad I was that I would soon be gone!

I stood at the door for a long time after the men had gone, thinking what I must do. The Trenton man, Mr. Tolivar, was to return by next morning. That left me but one day to do as I had promised. Perhaps it was only then that the enormity of my undertaking came to heart. But as I stood there, all but transfixed, I recalled that the girl was waiting for me to bring her food. That immediate necessity set me free.

I returned to the house. The boy was still sitting silently, hands folded in his lap. He said nothing, but I knew he was waiting for information.

"Have they gone?" came Mistress Shinn's voice from the back room.

"Yes," I said, going to the door where she was. "Mister Shinn told me that I was to work in the western field. I'll take some food and spend the day."

"I'll get it for thee if thee can wait," she called.

"I'll do it myself," I replied. Hurriedly I went to the pantry. I took up a whole loaf of bread, and some cheese, and filled my pockets with dried apple bits.

"She's safe," I whispered across the room to the boy. Then I raced outside, going as fast as possible northward to Morgan's Rock.

When I reached the river I found it somewhat lower, certainly much less swift than it had been before.

Not caring if I got wet or not, I waded in. The water was no higher now than my chest. In moments I found the girl, waiting for me. Hungrily she took the food.

"I spoke with your friend," I told her, watching her eat.

"Is he all right?"

"I told him I'd free him, too."

She stopped eating. "I thank you," she said gratefully.

"Your master—that Mister Tolivar—will be here tomorrow to fetch him," I told her. "You must be gone by then. And I should warn you that they're still searching for you. You must stay hidden."

"Will you still help us get away?" she asked between gulps of food.

"I'll try."

"Then we'll be safe," she said, with more assurance than I had.

"It will have to be tonight," I warned her. "Be patient. I'll try to come one more time today, but I may not be able to. Don't worry if I can't. I'll come at night, and bring your friend. But, remember, they're still looking. Do you understand that?"

She nodded.

"How is your arm?" I asked her.

"It will be fine," she said with a shrug.

I wanted to tell her then that I planned to join them in their flight, but suddenly I was afraid she might say no, so I held back. "Does it give you any pain?" I asked instead.

"No," she answered.

Quickly, then, I left the island, going directly to the work that Mr. Shinn had set for me. All day I kept thinking of what was to be done, more and more certain of its rightness. Only one thing worried me: What would happen if Mr. Shinn guessed and attempted to bar our way?

2

That afternoon, tired and hungry, I returned from the field. I had not eaten since early morning. Moreover, I had worked diligently, so the fact that I had gone to Morgan's Rock in the morning to see the girl would not be evident from the amount of work I had done. My arm began to ache again.

Throughout the day I tried to plan out how I would proceed that evening. But I had yet to concoct a thing.

I was thinking through it all once again when, as I approached the house, I discovered that Mr. Shinn had returned and was waiting for me in front of the house. I had passed my hours assuming the girl was safe simply because the search party had gone south. Seeing him there made me realize that it might be otherwise.

My first reaction was of alarm. "Did you find her?"

I called out as soon as he was in hailing distance, realizing as soon as I had spoken that it was wrong to have done so.

He shook his head. "It's not likely either," he acknowledged when I came closer. "She's either still in Jersey, as thee suggested, or has come across like the boy and is gone. It wasn't for want of looking that we failed."

"I've been to the field as you asked me to," I let him know.

"I thank thee," he said.

Not wanting to discuss the matter further, I started to pass him by. As I was going he put his arm before me, preventing me from going.

"Peter," he said quietly and with obvious difficulty, "I'm not sorry she has gone. I've no stomach for it. This John Tolivar will come for the boy in the morning. I'll not be easy until I ask him to set the boy free. I doubt, however, he'll do it. Even so, I'll take none of the reward money."

I didn't know why he wanted me to know these thoughts. I could only guess he wanted to soothe his guilt. But nothing that he could have said was more calculated to make me angry. There he talked of *persuading* the master to free the boy, while he himself held him prisoner! Only with an effort did I hold my tongue.

At dinner the boy sat at the table with us. When Mr. Shinn spoke the prayer, the boy did not even bow his head. Mr. Shinn noticed this, began a rebuke, but refrained. My admiration was for the boy.

The meal was a silent one. Only once did Mr. Shinn speak. "For what crime," he asked the boy, "were thee transported?"

"I wanted to keep my friend from prison," he replied.

"By what right did thee presume to do so?"

The boy said nothing; he only stared in his plate. Mr. Shinn repeated his question, demanding an answer.

"A prison is an awful place," the boy finally replied. "I would wish no one there."

"Then thee know of them thyself."

"My father is a debtor and is retained there."

Mr. Shinn said no more. His wife tried to be more cheerful, but no one caught her forced spirit, and she let off. Before we were done, it felt as dull inside as it was out.

When the meal was completed, Mr. Shinn turned to the boy. "I'm afraid," he said, "that thee must go to the building."

The boy stood without protest.

"Are thee comfortable there?" Mr. Shinn asked. "Were thee cold last night?"

The boy shook his head.

Furious, I jumped from the table and started for the loft. Before I reached the ladder, Mr. Shinn called out, "Peter will lead you back."

I stood where I was.

"Peter York," repeated Mr. Shinn, "did thee hear me?"

"I did," I returned, but stood, unmoving, determined not to do this thing for him.

"Do as I have asked thee," he repeated, his face turning red.

Losing my temper, I spun about. "It's your prison, not mine! I've no stomach for it!" I shouted, using his own words.

His face blazing with anger, he lifted his hand as if to strike me. But even as he did so, his other hand, as if from a different person, caught his upraised wrist, and so he restrained himself.

Frightened by his anger, my will gave way. I went out the door where I waited for the boy. When he followed I led the way down the path. I went before him slowly, shamed to have been so used.

When I reached the outbuilding, I opened the door and waited for him to go in. I realized I had to say something, yet did not know what to speak.

The boy went to the back of the place and sat down, his eyes upon me.

"Mister Shinn said they are coming for me tomorrow," he said. It was not a question, but I knew he was asking one all the same.

"Yes," I said lamely. "You must go tonight."

"Have you seen her?" he asked.

"This morning," I told him. "I said you'd join her. I'll come for you tonight, as soon as it's safe," I concluded abruptly, then shut the door and fastened the hasp.

Instead of returning to the house, I went to the barn. I watered and fed Jumper, realizing there was no way I could take her with me. She would be too likely to give us away. More, I worried that if I did take her, it might be considered theft. I wanted no part of that, though it pained me that Mr. Shinn would gain her through my going. I bid her a hasty goodbye.

Emerging from the barn, I saw Mr. Shinn standing in the doorway of the house. He was outlined by the light from within. Had he watched me as I talked to the boy? I wondered. His face was impassive as ever.

I passed him without either of us saying a word. Inside, I took up my boots and worked them with grease, for they were tight and uncomfortable. I knew it would be a long while before I would be able to treat them again.

In time Mr. Shinn came in and sat before the fire, but such thoughts as he had, he kept to himself.

Mistress Shinn, meanwhile, was across the room reading to her children in a low voice. The loudest noise was the burning fire. The air was thick and heavy, all too warm.

"Some of those searching are still not satisfied," Mr. Shinn pronounced to no one in particular. "They still think they can catch the girl."

I stopped working on my boots.

"I thought they had given up," Mistress Shinn answered him.

"The reward's too high," Mr. Shinn continued. "They feel they've nothing to lose by looking. Robert Pall, for one, is convinced she's still about, the more so now that the river's dropped so much."

"Will thee go with them?" his wife asked.

"I've met my obligation," he returned heavily. "Mister Pall thinks she might have gone north, rather than south as Peter suggested. He intends to try that way tonight."

"I had thought Robert Pall a wiser man," said Mistress Shinn. "To consider such a thing! No one's likely to cross the river at night."

"Aye," repeated Mr. Shinn. "It's the money."

Though the conversation had not been meant for me, I well understood its import. If my plan had been hard before, it became thrice so now. I could only console myself with the thought I did not care if I were caught and brought trouble on Mr. Shinn.

After a while Mr. Shinn fetched his Bible, which he laid on his knees, and began to read. In time, he began to read out loud. I had no ear for it—not from him—and continued with my boots.

"Peter," he broke off to say. "Thee should listen."

I stood up. "Forgive me," I said pertly enough. "I'm too tired." And without waiting for permission, I bade them a good night and climbed into the loft.

I had no intention of sleeping. I doubt I could have even if I had chosen to. I was far too tense. I started at everything. For example, I noticed that Mistress Shinn had returned my britches from the day before. Folded and clean, they lay beside my bedding. They were better than what I had on, so I changed into them. But as I did so I suddenly stopped, remembering something: Mr. Shinn's linen handkerchief, the one I had used to try to stop the girl's bleeding! Had I put it in my britches pocket or had I lost it? Searching the britches, I found nothing. I decided it must have been lost and my fears were only nervousness.

I listened to them below. The children were sent to their beds. Soon Mistress Shinn went to her room, leaving Mr. Shinn alone. Hastily I lay on my bedding and pulled the blanket over me.

For a long while I heard him pacing about. I knew him well enough to know he was working thoughts through his mind. How I wished I knew them!

Then I heard his foot on the ladder rung. Ducking

my head under the blanket, I arranged it so that I could peer out with one eye. Sure enough, he came up, candle in hand. He looked about, making certain I was asleep. Satisfied, he went back down.

Throwing off the blanket, I watched the glow of his candle from above. He walked about some more, then there was silence until I heard the low murmuring of his ardent prayers. At last the candle went out, and everything grew dark and still.

Listening to every sound, I tried to make myself wait. After I waited as long as I was able, I slipped from my place and started slowly down the ladder, pausing to listen and search about with every step I took.

In moments I was on the floor. At the end of the room the hearth fire still glowed, casting a dull red light. I glanced about to see if there was anything I could take, but decided to take nothing.

With the greatest caution I pulled the door open. It came without noise. Again I listened. There was nothing but the diminished rolling of the river. I shut the door behind me.

I had left the house.

3

For a long time I stood motionless, uncertain, even afraid now that I had actually begun what I had sworn to do. I found, despite my early resolution, that it was necessary to argue, push, and exhort myself, reminding myself again that what I was about to do was right. I sensed well that what hovered underneath was an indecision about my going. In truth, I think if I had been prevented then from going farther my inner heart might have rejoiced. But I was shamed to have such thoughts.

How long I stood before Mr. Shinn's house I do not know. The air was clear and warm, warmer than the ground, as often happens in early spring. The low grounds were swollen with fog, a fog that came and went like passing fancies. Above, a half-moon rose to brilliance, bringing just enough white light to let me see my way while making the dew on every tree twig luminescent. The stars, overwhelmed by the moon, were few in number, but those that remained seemed each a spying eye.

With a final heavy effort I turned toward the outbuilding where I knew the boy was waiting, making my way slowly. At the door again I paused, knowing full well that beyond this point there could be no more hesitations. If I opened this door and bade the boy come out, I would be considered as guilty as those who ran away. I sought to mouth some prayers but could find no words.

Holding the moment, I listened. All was still save my heart and the softer river. Momentarily I thought I heard the door of the big house behind me. I strained, but decided it was naught.

Opening the shed door I made a sound.

"Who's there?" the boy nervously asked out of the dark.

"Peter," I answered in a whisper.

"Are we going now?" he asked.

"Yes."

"Where?" he wanted to know.

"To Elizabeth first," I told him.

"I'll follow," he returned.

As we went by the house I paused. It bulked large but still. Again I thought I heard a noise. The notion that Mr. Shinn had been feigning sleep and was coming to arrest us came to mind. But nothing happened, and we passed on.

Roads at night seem always newly made. What was most familiar to me became, in that semidarkness, unknown. I had to stop and look, to study everything that came before me as if I were a foreigner to the land. I listened too, cautious of all sounds, recalling only too well what Mr. Shinn had said about the search party. No doubt they were about, though of where they were, I had no idea.

"Do you not know the way?" the boy asked when I remained unmoving, perplexed at my stillness for a particularly long time.

"I think we'd better go along the river," I replied. Catching the river's sound, I determined the way and started off in a new direction.

By going in that fashion we left what there was of any road, and our steps became greatly impeded. The fog, which seemed to come and go, made things worse. The dampness soaked us, chilled us. Nor could I keep myself from being fearful that we were making too much noise. I made us go even slower.

By day it might have taken us ten minutes to reach the river. That night it took us more. It felt like an hour. Throughout, the boy hardly spoke, only to assure me that he was close.

At one time I saw a spot of light. I assumed it was the search party, for it moved with many starts and stops. It came from the south of us, lasted but a short time, and finally disappeared. As glad as I was that it was at another place, it convinced me that searchers were indeed about. I redoubled our precautions, actually pausing between each step.

In time we reached the river's edge. The rapidly lapping water with its steady flow spread before us.

It was impossible to see across. The fog, heaviest here, covered the river, making night and water one.

"Is she far?" the boy asked.

"Not very," I returned, though in truth I was not at all certain where we were.

We continued north, our feet—mine booted and his bare—sucking deep into the water-soaked shore. Our splashing seemed awfully loud to me. More than once I cautioned him to be more quiet. Never objecting, he tried to comply. But in his haste to keep with me, he constantly made more noise.

"If we're heard there will be no escape," I warned him anew.

We continued on, quieter, even more slowly than we had gone before.

I kept a constant watch but saw no more lights to suggest the search party was anywhere nearby. The thought that they had gone elsewhere was reassuring.

So fanciful was the fog that we reached the lower portion of Morgan's Rock before I truly realized where we were. When I did perceive it I said nothing to the boy until we came fully abreast of it. Then I stopped. "There," I whispered. "On that island. That's where she is."

He drew closer and I could hear his nervous, rapid breathing. How he guessed I never knew, but it was only then that he asked, "Is she hurt?"

"Aye," I admitted.

"How?" he asked.

Ashamed to say, I continued on in silence till we had reached the landing spot. "Can you swim?" I asked then.

"No," he told me. "Is it deep? Can't I walk?"

"You'd best remain here," I told him. "It may be too deep for you. I won't be able to manage the both of you. I'll go across quickly and bring her back."

"I'd rather go with you," he protested nervously.

"It can't be," I insisted. "You'll be safe enough here. I won't be long."

"I won't stay," he informed me with great urgency, clearly fearful of being left alone.

"I *won't* abandon you."

Ignoring me, he took hold of my arm and would not let go. I could have forced him to stay but was afraid of what he might do, particularly of the noise he could make. I gave way.

"Then do exactly as I say," I told him. "Hold to me tightly, walk carefully, and no matter what, don't let go or you'll be lost and beyond my help."

He placed his hands on my arm and gripped it.

We began to walk into the water. The outline of the island across the way, close as it was, was still dim. Carefully, testing the way with each step, we kept going till the water reached my waist. The current proved to be no problem.

"Are you all right?" I whispered.

"Yes," he answered.

We moved farther on, the shore behind us folding back into the fog. Midway we could see neither shore. The only noise was the water.

When the river reached my chest, the boy's feet could no longer reach the ground. He had to allow himself to be pulled. I went carefully, only hoping I would not fall into any holes.

In moments the water level began to drop, and the boy regained his footing. He began to move forward on his own. Unexpectedly he slipped and splashed down on his knees, giving out a cry. I leaped toward him. "Quiet!" I ordered, pulling him up.

The stillness resumed.

Holding him, I walked up on the island, then turned to look back. The fog had once more drawn in behind. It was as if the Pennsylvania shore had vanished.

4

Once on the island we had to find the girl. She did not, as I had hoped, reveal herself as soon as we came. That she was not where I had asked her to be made me grow anxious and unsure where to turn. My obvious concern and hesitancy made the boy more nervous than he was before.

"Where is she?" he demanded, as much an accusation as a question.

"Be patient," I said, trying to calm him. "She's about."

Throughly alarmed he wheeled about. "Elizabeth!" he cried.

"Be quiet!" I begged him. "We'll be heard!"

He would not be persuaded. "Elizabeth!" he called again, his voice rising with his agitation.

In despair of his folly I ran from him toward the bushes in the hope of finding the girl quickly, only to be rewarded by a crackling of steps from yet another place. The boy stumbled toward that, calling, "It's me, Robert!" To my great relief I saw—in such light as there was—the girl emerge from her hiding place. In seconds they were together.

I stood apart and watched them as they whispered to one another. Greatly nervous about all the noise that had been made, and more than anxious to be gone, I came up to them. "We must hurry," I begged them.

Once they were together they continued to stay close. Never in what subsequently happened did they make any decision without silent nods and agreements between themselves. It was not that they discussed things. They did not seem to need that; nevertheless, they reached a common understanding and acted as one.

"We'll have to go across again," I told them. "Once we're on the other side I'll lead you north. The farther we go, the safer you'll be."

We went to the island's shore. Standing between them, I bade them both cling to me, to walk when they could and allow themselves to be carried when they could not. "Just don't hold me back," I warned. This they seemed to understand.

Once again we returned to the water, moving away from Morgan's Rock as I had done so many times before, but now with two people clinging to me, one on either side.

As if each gave life to the other, they moved quicker and with greater sureness than before. The sensation that they might soon be free seemed to renew their strength. A new urgency was in their walk.

We pushed on quickly, unmindful, I fear, of how much sound we made, splashing loudly. Our sole intent was the safety of the Pennsylvania shore.

Soon the water grew too deep for the boy and then for the girl. As I had told them, they clung to me while I breasted those few deep feet until the girl called out, "I can touch!" In a moment the boy announced the same, and we all walked toward the shore, which began to define itself out of the confusion of the fog.

We had reached a depth no greater than my knees, and were no more perhaps than four or five yards from the shore, when a crashing burst out before us, and great forms sprang up.

"Stand!" came an order. Someone attempted to strike a light.

Who it was I could not see, but I needed no further understanding. We had been discovered by the search party. As one, we leaped toward the south, running through the water along the shore's edge.

"Stop!" came the command behind us. "Stop or we'll shoot!"

"Run!" I shouted at the other two as we raced along, not even certain if both were there.

A gunshot boomed behind us, but whether it was shot into the air or aimed badly, I don't know. No one was struck, but it added a frenzy to our dash.

Now, from behind, came the men, shouting and leaping through the river after us. It proved an advantage. We could see their lantern and hear their shouts. We, for all our crashing, remained within the dark.

"Stop!" came the repeated calls. "By order of the law, stop!"

We paid them no heed, but continued to run, I in the lead, now fairly pulling the other two. As I ran I realized the danger in our running south. It was in that direction that I had earlier seen a light. Were we being pushed toward another force?

Instantly I understood what we had to do. "Out of the river," I called to them, and yanking, hauled them up on the shore. The girl, caught off step, stumbled, crying out. The boy stopped to help her, even as I kept pulling, urging them to hurry, seeking the protection of the bushes, the trees, the fog— anything to hide us from view.

Our pursuers drew much closer.

"Here!" I called to my companions, pushing them down about me in the well of some bushes. "Be quiet. No sounds!"

No sounds. The three of us, pressed together, struggling for breath, sounded nothing less than a thunderstorm to me. Fortunately our noise was nothing compared to that of the searchers. We heard them plainly enough on the river, floundering, shouting orders to one another in great confusion. They understood soon enough that we had left the river, though at what place they could not tell.

The three of us remained crouched in place, resisting the strong temptation to bolt. Desperately I tried to decide how many searchers there were, where they might look for us, and what we could next do.

For all their sounds, they could have numbered a

hundred. In fact, there were never more than three. Even so, we felt surrounded. They stomped here, there, everywhere, tearing apart whatever impeded them or whatever they thought might be concealing us. At one point they came so close I could hear their labored breath as well as their hushed voices.

Huddled together in as tight a ring as we could manage, neither talking nor moving, we waited. In this the other two were far better practiced than I. How my body ached!

In wider and wider circles the searching men tried in vain to find us. At times I was sure they had gone away. But, just when I was almost certain we were free to move, they would return, and once more we were compelled to stay.

It was not the staying that I feared, but the fact that we might have to wait too long. With the day would come the light. Then they could find us at their leisure. We could not wait.

Nevertheless, we stayed in our hiding place for more than an hour, perhaps two. Sometimes we relaxed, only to start at a noise. In time, however, our patience was rewarded. All grew absolutely quiet.

"Do you think they're gone?" asked the boy.

So it seemed. Once again, only the river sounds were heard.

I made bold to stand. The capricious fog had

drifted off. It was darker too. The moon had shifted down.

"Can we go?" the girl asked.

I listened once more. "I think so," I replied.

"Do you know where we are?" whispered the boy.

I did not. I didn't know how far south we had come, how deep into the woods we had gone. I only knew we hadn't crossed River Road. That was my choice.

"We need to find the road," I said, sounding as certain as I could.

"Is it safe?" asked the girl.

Again we listened. Nothing. No sounds.

"Yes," I finally said.

They stood with me. Such light as remained could hardly find its way between the web of trees and shrubs. I tried to get a sense of where we were. I could place nothing but the river, but that at least informed me of one direction *not* to go.

"This way," I quietly said.

We began to move at random, though I wanted to make it seem as if I knew just where to go. Most of all I tried to keep the river behind us. Thus we stepped our way.

Only once did we think we heard the men again, but the noise we heard drew from the south. It served to reassure us. On we went. I tried to make a decision as to the best way to go, though in truth I could think no farther than River Road. I had first to find that road.

That goal my guiding thought, we stumbled all but blindly with me in the lead, the two holding to one another and, by turns, to me. More than once I thought we had reached the road but found only an empty clearing.

"Is it very far?" asked the girl, sounding weary.

"I think not," I answered without sure knowledge.

We continued some way farther, only to all but fall upon the road. I sensed it at once. A feeling of openness stretched out on all sides. We could even see the stars, for now that the moon was down, they were brighter than before.

At the road we paused, both to make sure the path was clear and to give the girl a rest.

"Is it your arm?" I asked her.

"No," she answered.

But I knew it was.

I told them that the road was the best route to take because it would lead at length to Easton. Just how many miles that would be I was not sure. Perhaps as much as forty.

Pronouncing herself ready again, the girl got up and we moved on. Our way was easier, which was a blessing. No obstruction marred our path. A sense of release opened out our spirits.

But even as they began to sense their freedom, my tension grew. I had yet to tell them I was prepared to join them. Seeing how they clung to one another, I began to wonder if they would in fact accept me. Yet again, I was not truly certain what I wanted: for them to refuse me or to accept me. I dared not know my mind.

We continued northward for two or three miles, staying close to the side of the road, when the sound of something different caught my ear. Instantly I stood still, bidding the others not to move.

I heard it again. Unmistakably, it was the sound of a horse striking the ground with its hoof—once, twice, three times.

From where we stood I could not tell if it was a horse at pasture or one with a rider. Deciding to be prudent, I told the two to take themselves off the road and wait while I went forward to reconnoiter. This they agreed to do. Reminding them to hold their voices, I crept forward cautiously.

Slowly I walked up the road, prepared to flee if necessary. In moments I saw an open field. There, silhouetted in the dim light, stood a horse by a tree. I stopped where I was and looked. Something about the horse arrested my attention. I was sure I knew it. Moving a little closer I realized that the horse had a saddle on its back. I peered again, understanding at last. The horse was Jumper.

The moment I recognized the mare, I spun about. Too late! The shape of a man stood between me and where I had left the others.

"Peter York?" inquired a voice. "Is that thee?"

It was Mr. Shinn.

5

He stood but ten feet ahead of me. I could hardly see his face, but I recognized his form as I'm sure he recognized mine. Thus we remained, staring not so much at one another as at the darkness that lay between.

"Does thee have both of them with thee?" he spoke at last.

"I'll not say," I replied.

"Did the search party see thee?" he said after a moment.

"I don't know."

"Peter," he said with urgency, "the law says thee are equally guilty if thee help a bondsman escape."

"I don't care."

He sighed. "Will thee show me where the boy is?"

"I told you, no."

"Why?"

"You'll only return him to his master," I charged. "You said it was the law."

"The law is necessary, Peter," he replied with new emotion.

"Let me go!" I shouted out at him.

"I'm not holding thee," he said softly.

"They're waiting for me," I fairly begged. "They need me!"

"Peter York," he said, "*I'm not holding thee*."

"But will you hinder me?" I cried.

"I'm not holding thee," he said once again.

I stood there, not knowing what he meant to do but afraid to go one way or the other. Impulsively I took a step forward and started to walk past him. He held out an arm to block my way.

"Thy horse," he whispered close to my ear. "Thee has forgotten thy horse."

I looked up at him but could see nothing but the dim outline of his face.

"I don't understand you!" I cried in vexation.

"Get *thy* horse," he repeated.

"Tell me what you want of me!" I shouted.

"Get *thy* horse," he returned in even tones.

"*My* horse." I threw the words back at him. "Why can't you say your meaning?!"

"*Thy* horse," he only repeated in his soft voice.

Exasperated and close to tears, I turned about and

walked toward the tree where Jumper stood. Calling to her softly, I saw that she recognized me. I untied the rope that held her, then pulled myself up on her back.

Touching her flanks with my heels I moved down the road where Mr. Shinn remained. I paused in front of him, still waiting for him to do something.

But he only stood there.

Though I was unsure whether he was tricking me by getting me to bring out the runaways, I began to think he might not stop us. I had no choice but to take a chance.

Urging Jumper on, I trotted down the road to where the two were waiting.

"Robert! Elizabeth!" I called. But they, startled by the loud voices, at first refused to come. "It's me, Peter," I called to them. "Hurry, please."

My name brought them clamoring to know where the horse came from, if I had stolen it, who the man was, and many other questions, all of which I refused to answer. I urged them to hurry.

One after the other I helped them up behind me.

"Listen carefully," I cautioned when they both sat behind me. "I don't know what he intends."

"Who is it?" demanded the girl.

"It doesn't matter," I said. "But if he tries to stop us, I'll leap off. You must then go on without me as fast as you can. I won't let him stop you."

"Why, what will he do?" asked the boy nervously.

"Do as I say," I said brusquely to hide my own fear.

Not waiting any longer, I turned Jumper's head and urged her up the road.

As we went I leaned forward, trying to see what Mr. Shinn was doing. At first I could not tell. But as we drew closer I saw him clearly enough: he was standing in the middle of the road, standing absolutely still.

I pulled the horse to a stop.

"What is it?" whispered the boy.

Instead of answering, I passed the reins back to them and placed myself so that I could jump down on Mr. Shinn if he made the slightest move to impede the horse. Then I urged Jumper on, slowly. As we drew closer, Mr. Shinn waited, unmoving.

In a moment we drew abreast of him. In spite of myself I made the horse stop, and then, touching the horse, passed him by. He gave one quick look up at us. No more.

When we had gone on a few yards, I stopped and looked back. He was still standing, his back to us, in the middle of the road.

"Up!" I shouted to Jumper, and threw her into a gallop down the road.

They had their freedom. But in that same moment, I knew I did not want mine.

6

For most of the night we rode along though never again at the speed with which we had begun. Instead, we kept a steady pace, but at a far greater rate than we could have walked. Sometimes the boy slept, but not she, nor I. The farther we rode, the more certain I was that they were safe and not pursued. In time I knew they were completely free. It was then I halted.

"I can't go any farther," I said. "You're safe enough. I think you can go wherever you want." So saying, I slipped down from Jumper.

They started to jump off as well, but I prevented that.

"The horse is yours," I told them. "It's mine to give and I give it freely. I don't want it. It's been a burden to me."

They both protested strongly, but I was stronger yet, telling them I owed them no less. My eyes, rather than my words, were trying to say it was for the hurt I'd done Elizabeth. She said nothing then but in time they agreed to take the mare.

"Where will you go?" I asked.

"We were told we could hire our labor in Easton," the boy said.

"And if you can't?" I wondered.

"We will," insisted the girl through her tiredness.

"I think so too," I felt compelled to say, joining my wish to theirs.

"Are you going home?" she asked.

I nodded, yes.

"Will it be hard for you when you get there?" the boy wanted to know.

"I can't say," I answered truthfully.

"Why don't you come with us," suddenly suggested the girl. "It will be better with the three of us. We're not much good in country, but in town, we'll be able to take care of you." As she spoke she reached down to touch me. "I've no anger against you," she let me know, and I knew then she had not even told the boy what I'd done.

"No," I replied, shaking my head. "I must go back."

"Are you sure?"

"No," I admitted. "But I must."

Wanting them to be gone, I made the farewells as brief as was seemly. In time they went. I watched them until they were hidden by the dark.

For a moment I almost ran after them. Not for the thoughts or reasons I had had before, but because I was fearful of what would happen to me when I returned. Nonetheless, I turned about and started back.

I walked as long as I could for the rest of the night and into the morning. I passed but one rider, no one

I knew, and it was a strange relief to have him as indifferent to me as I was to him.

Then, exhausted and unable to go farther, I found a somewhat protected spot by the side of the road. There I lay down. Cradling my head I tried desperately to think what would be done to me on my return. Before I had reached any conclusions I fell asleep.

I woke in late afternoon. For a while I lay in a dreamy state of semislumber. Then, hearing a noise I rolled over. A few feet from me sat Mr. Shinn. He had yet to notice that I was awake.

I looked at him carefully. He was no different than I had known him before. Still, he struck me as older, heavier. His pale face and gray hair appeared duller than I had remembered, more bleached of life. His eyes were searching off someplace, I knew not where.

Only when I made a noise did he shift his glance. We looked at each other.

"Thee has slept some," he said at last.

"How long have you been here?" I asked.

He shrugged his heavy shoulders.

"Did you catch them?" I asked suddenly, alarmed.

He shook his head. "Nay, Peter. I did not even try. Where's thy horse?"

"I gave the horse to them," I replied after a moment.

"Did thee? Why?"

"I didn't want her," I said. "She belonged to something else."

He nodded as if he understood but said no more. I studied him. Clearly he was working something in his mind. I wondered what it was and when he would speak. More than once he started, only to stop. At last he found his tongue.

"Peter York," he began, "thee has spoken and acted for me when I—when I as your elder should have so done. Thee were right and I was wrong. I did not have the strength thee had." He bowed his head. "I needed thee—who art no more than a boy—to act for me. I, Everett Shinn, thank thee humbly."

"Did you know what I was going to do?" I asked, amazed.

"Aye," he said, looking at me again. "Thee gave many signs. Thee does not lie well."

"You knew I was going to free the boy?"

"I wanted thee to do so."

"But you asked me to search for the girl!" I cried.

"Only so you could lead them away from her."

"They almost caught us last night," I said.

"I tried to keep them to the south of where thee were, south of Morgan's Rock. I followed thee out and even showed a light. I did the best I could."

"Does anybody else know what I've done?" I asked.

"I think not. They might suspect, but no one has said as much."

"Do we have to tell them?" I wanted to know.

"I think we must," he said.

"It will do you harm," I cried.

"Perhaps a greater good," he concluded, standing up as if to go.

I held back. "I meant to go with them."

"I thought thee would. Why?"

"I could not abide by what you were doing."

He shifted uneasily before me. "Peter York," he said, "I have said the wrong I did. What was the gunshot that brought me to thee yesterday?"

"I shot her," I said in a very low voice. "In the arm. Did you know?"

It was then he pulled the linen handkerchief from his pocket for me to see. It was stained with blood. "When Mistress Shinn found it, I feared that thee had killed," he said, his voice breaking.

We looked at one another.

"What will thee do now, Peter York?" he asked.

"I wish to return home."

"Aye," he agreed. "We can reach it by tonight. It will be late, for the road is poor. But I think we can do it. Are thee ready?"

"Yes."

He held out his hand to help me up. I rose, but instead of stepping back from him, I put my arms about him. He did the same to me. We stood that way in silence.

"I was afraid you would not want me," I cried.

"Aye," he echoed, "I feared the same of thee."

It would be dark before we arrived home. No matter. Together we knew the way.

JOIN IN ALL THE FUN WITH THE KIDS FROM SOUTH ORANGE RIVER SCHOOL

S.O.R. LOSERS

69993-1/$4.99 US/$6.99 Can

The South Orange River (S.O.R.) School is big on sports and famous for not losing a game all season. That all changes when the school insists that some seventh-grader non-jocks form a soccer team. The new team is sure that losing their first game 32-0 will put an end to their athletic adventure, but no such luck. Their parents insist they try harder. The whole school cheers them on, and they finally score . . . for the other team. And only the eleven members of the *S.O.R. Losers* team know the sceret of their outstanding "success."

ROMEO AND JULIET TOGETHER (AND ALIVE!) AT LAST

70525-7/$4.99 US/$6.99 Can

Pete Saltz, the pudgy poet from *S.O.R. LOSERS*, has fallen hard for Anabell Stackpoole, and she likes him too. But both are much too shy to do anything about it.

It's Pete's friend Ed Sitrow to the rescue, as he and other eighth graders at South Orange River School cook up a scheme to give the budding romance a boost. It's a school production of *Romeo and Juliet*, with the bashful pair in the leading roles—and eveybody's waiting for the kissing scenes. What they get is more action than Shakespeare ever imagined, in the funniest, most disastrous . . . and most romantically successful production ever!

AV1 0999

AVI

REMARKABLE STORIES OF

BLUE HERON
72043-4/$4.50 US/$6.50 Can

At the start of a month-long vacation with her father, Maggie wonders why he is acting so strangely, making secretive calls and giving way to angry outbursts.

Then in the marsh, Maggie discovers a majestic heron that appears to have a magic all its own. But she discovers someone else has been watching the heron and this person wishes to kill it.

As Maggie struggles to find a way to save her father *and* the heron, she begins to sense a connection between all these events.

A PLACE CALLED UGLY
72423-5/$4.99 US/$6.99 Can

There's no reasoning with Owen. The island cottage where he and his family have spent the last ten summers *must* be preserved. Never mind that a bulldozer is ready to level the place and Owen's family is hurrying to catch the last ferry—or that *nobody* sees it his way. Alone, fourteen-year-old Owen is going to stay and save the beautiful place others call ugly.

GROWING UP AND SELF-DISCOVERY

SOMETIMES I THINK
I HEAR MY NAME
72424-3/$4.50 US/$6.50 Can

It wasn't that thirteen-year-old Conrad didn't like living with his aunt and uncle in St. Louis. It's just that his mother and father live in New York and he hadn't seen them lately. That's how Conrad happened to spend a strange week in New York City with a girl he hardly knew—getting more answers than he had questions . . . about his parents, himself and what real families are all about.

PUNCH WITH JUDY
72253-4/$4.50 US/$5.99 Can

Punch is a starving orphan when he's rescued from the streets by the owner of a traveling medicine show. Punch doesn't mind what he does, as long as he can cast his love-sick gaze on Judy, the owner's beautiful daughter. But then the owner dies and Judy tries to keep the show going despite smaller audiences, a morally outraged preacher, and a sheriff determined to arrest them. And when the law closes in on them, it's Punch's chance to perform—and to save the day.

AV4 0999

TERRIFYING TALES OF

THE MAN WHO WAS POE
71192-3/$4.99 US/$6.99 Can

Edmund is all alone in 19th-century Providence. His mother is gone, and his aunt, who went in search of her, is dead. Even his sister has disappeared under mysterious circumstances.

Through a chance encounter, Edmund enlists the help of a dark, mysterious stranger who calls himself Auguste Dupin. But is Dupin, in reality the tormented author Edgar Allan Poe? And is he really interested in helping Edmund find his sister, or does he view Edmund's plight as the source of a new story to write—one with a tragic ending?

"WHO WAS THAT MASKED MAN, ANYWAY?"
72113-9/$3.99 US/$4.99 Can

A super pilot is being chased by giants, a master spy searches for his true identity, an invisible hero single-handedly fights the forces of evil . . . and Frankie is falling into big trouble for living in the daring world of radio adventure—instead of getting his homework done! Will Frankie escape the punishment of his parents and teacher? Will his magic decoder ring save him? Tune in tomorrow to discover Frankie's fate.

MYSTERY AND SUSPENSE

SOMETHING UPSTAIRS
70853-1/$4.99 US/$6.50 Can

"This is the strangest story I've ever heard . . . I think it's true."
Avi

It rose from the dark stain on the floor . . . A white glow, almost shiny, filled the windowless space. Two hands, then two arms, reached up from the stain. Kenny stood staring. It was beyond belief.

A head rose up from the stain, then came a neck. The humanlike shape radiated a soft, pale, pulsing glow. Its hand reached out toward Kenny, beckoning him, luring him with the unknown horror that haunted the room, ensnaring him in an unspeakable history from which he might never escape.

WINDCATCHER
71805-7/$4.99 US/$6.99 Can

When Tony is out maneuvering in his sailboat among the offshore islands, he comes across a mysterious couple in a high-powered motorboat.

Tony does some investigating on his own and what he discovers leads him on a daring hunt for a 200-year-old shipwreck . . . and a dangerous confrontation with treasure hunters who will stop at nothing to keep Tony from learning their secret.

THE BARN

72562-2/$4.99 US/$7.50 Can

The schoolmaster says nine-year-old Benjamin is the finest student he's ever seen—fit for more than farming; destined for great things someday. But his father's grave illness brings Ben home from school and compels him to strive for something great *right now*—to do the one thing that will please Father so much he'll want to live. But first Ben must convince his older sister and brother to work with him. And together, they succeed in ways they never dreamed possible.

"A knockout story!"
Chicago Tribune

"A vivid picture of time and place . . .
a thought-provoking and engaging piece
of historical fiction."
School Library Journal

Booklist Editors' Choice
ALA Notable Book
American Bookseller Pick of the Lists
Chicago Tribune Best Book for Young Readers
Teachers' Choice 1995

00011851

AV6 0999